# TALES of THE FRIENDSHIP BENCH

## A Novel

### (Book 4 of the Gumbeaux Sistahs series)

## JAX FREY

Tales of the Friendship Bench

Printed in the United States of America
First Printing 2022

ISBN paperback: 978-1-7331582-3-7

Cover Illustration: Friendship Bench by Jax Frey

Dedicated to my friend, Ellen LaRocca—
a true Gumbeaux Sistah

# FRIENDSHIP

In everyone's life, at some time, our inner fire goes out. It is then burst into flame by an encounter with another human being. We should all be thankful for those people who rekindle the inner spirit.

—Albert Schweitzer

It's the friends you can call up at 4 a.m. that matter.

—Marlene Dietrich

The only way to have a friend is to be one.

—Ralph Waldo Emerson

A good friend knows all your stories. A best friend helped you create them.

—Unknown

A friend is someone who gives you total freedom to be yourself.

—Jim Morrison

Friendship isn't a big thing—it's a million little things.

—Paulo Coelho

We've been friends for so long I can't remember which one of us is the bad influence.

—Unknown

Many people will walk in and out of your life,
but only true friends will leave footprints on your heart.
—Eleanor Roosevelt

# LIST OF CHARACTERS

## Original Gumbeaux Sistahs:

**Judith Lafferty**: artist, single and co-owner, along with Dawn Berard, of The Gumbeaux Sistahs Gallery

**Dawn Berard**: co-owner of The Gumbeaux Sistahs Gallery and owner of family business Berard Accounting. Was married to Dan Berard, now widowed.

**Lola Broussard**: landscaper, lawyer, activist, best friends with Dawn and married twice to same man, Bud Broussard

**Bea Walker**: retired, widow, unofficial leader of the Gumbeaux Sistahs, lay minister with the Episcopal Church, co-creator of the Friendship Bench

**Helen Hoffmann**: owner of Body Workings Essential Oils Company, nutrition expert, Reiki practitioner, widow, co-creator of the Friendship Bench

## Additional Gumbeaux Sistahs:

**Trinity Hebert**: newly added Gumbeaux Sistah and Dawn's younger sister, owner of Royal Gala Art Gallery in New Orleans

## Other Characters:

**Cooper Landry**: Helen's foster child, art student

**Zoe Abadie**: Dawn's Granddaughter, student, works with Lola in her landscaping business

**Chuck Bennett**: Cooper's Art teacher

**Jenny Matheson**: Bonnie Phillips daughter

**Gladys Percy**: Mrs. Melrose's housekeeper

**Sharon Brown**: owner of Natchez Coffee Company

## Visitors to the Friendship Bench

**Maddie Melrose**
**Gladys Percy**
**Sissy Etheridge**
**Bonnie Phillips**
**Linda Langley**
**Dolores Benedict**

# FORWARD

Dear Sistahs:

If you've been reading the Gumbeaux Sistahs novels, then you've probably figured out by now that the word "Gumbeaux" has come to mean so much more to me than a hot Cajun soup/stew concoction over rice, served sometimes with potato salad. Gumbeaux also means a lifestyle that includes close friends, family, connection, fulfillment, purpose, and sometimes, yes, even that beloved dish in a bowl.

Some people already have a version of this lifestyle, and to you I say—Gumbeaux down, girl! But unfortunately, some do not. And because it can add so much to your life, I want to encourage you to check out the Gumbeaux Sistahs website— www.gumbeauxsistahs. com —and consider forming your own Gumbeaux Sistahs group.

For those of you who already have a group of friends, the website can supply your group with suggested fun and meaningful activities that can draw you closer, get the hilarity started, and inspire you in your lives. Please consider inviting someone outside of your group to join you. They will only add color and it could help in the fight against loneliness.

For those of you in need of friends and a support group, the website will show you step-by-step how to get a Gumbeaux Sistahs group going quickly. Then you too can take advantage of the suggested activities.

It is my deepest wish to bring you sistahs closer together, help eliminate loneliness, connect you with your forever friends—and have a blast doing it.

Here's wishing y'all hot gumbo and cool friends—Gumbeaux on!

—JAX

**Oh my gravy! Now what?**
**—Judith**

# CHAPTER 1

"**O**h my gravy! Now what?" Judith Lafferty whispered to herself in disbelief. She sat on the bench in front of the Gumbeaux Sistahs Art Gallery, a business she owned with her partner, Dawn Berard. Judith's eyes were wide with wonder as she watched a tiny, older woman walk away from her down the sidewalk. Her name was Mrs. Melrose, and although she was diminutive and walked with a cane, she held herself erect and headed determinedly towards the black town car that was waiting for her. The driver hopped out to help her into the backseat. The woman looked back at Judith and called out warningly, "Remember! Two days!" When the car took off and passed Judith, Mrs. Melrose waived as if she were royalty in a coronation parade.

Judith sighed deeply and rubbed the ears of her pug dog Lucy, who was sitting next to the wooden bench where she sat. She needed some reassurance and her sweet dog was always good for it. The bench where she and her best friends, the Gumbeaux Sistahs, often sat offered comfort as well. They called the seat the Friendship Bench, and at this point, it was a bit of a downtown landmark in the small city of Covington, Louisiana. It had been installed a few years back in front of the gallery by two of the sistahs, Bea Walker and Helen Hoffmann, and it came with its own tradition. The sistahs took turns sitting on the bench on a regular schedule, and anyone who wished to do so could come and talk with them for a twenty-minute chat.

The subject of each chat was entirely up to the visitor. Sometimes they merely wanted a few minutes to talk to a friendly face and a kind listening ear. They might talk about their children, or about a brother in another city, or their favorite recipe for bread pudding. Sometimes a visitor wanted to talk to the sistahs about something they would never dream of talking about to their regular friends. For example, Dawn, another Sistah, once had a woman confess that she had a penchant for eating over a dozen beignets every day for breakfast. And Judith had listened to another woman talk about her unexpected crush on the local, married butcher. They couldn't very well trust one of their friend with that kind of sensitive information, but they felt they could trust a stranger on a bench. Then there were others who had more serious things to discuss. For example, there was the local librarian who found her husband cheating on her with a downtown beauty salon owner. That had been a tricky situation to handle, but the sistahs had managed.

Word had gotten around town about the Friendship Bench through word-of-mouth, and its popularity grew. So much so, the sistahs had installed two more benches and introduced several trusted friends to act as sitters there. At this point, the benches had helped dozens of people in the community and brought purpose and joy to the sistahs and the extended group of sitters.

Most often the sistahs just listened and acted as a friend to those who needed to talk. Then there were times when the sistahs referred people to local therapists. And once in a while, the sistahs encountered a visitor who had a problem that the sistahs simply did not know how to handle. To their credit, those were few and far between, but when it happened, they conferred with each other about the best course of action to take. This brings us back to Judith sitting on the bench. With a deep sigh and worried expression, she picked up her phone and texted, *"Emergency Bench Meeting tomorrow at noon at the gallery. I'll bring the gumbo!"*

**My doctor calls them booby traps!**
**—Judith**

# CHAPTER 2

The next morning, Dawn hurried into the Gumbeaux Sistahs Gallery and the other sistahs were waiting for her there. She muttered loudly, "This had better be good, Judith. I had to cancel a mammogram to be here." Dawn Berard, Judith's gallery partner, was a large woman who prided herself on her elegant clothes, jewelry, Cajun accent, and a penchant for sarcasm.

"Oh, I hate mammograms," said Judith. "My doctor calls them 'booby traps!'"

The sistahs broke out in good-humored laughter, and Lola Broussard, another sistah, spoke up, "Ooh that's the perfect name—it's just what they feel like."

Bea Walker was smiling, but said seriously "True, but they save lives, and that could include one of us someday, so make sure you reschedule." Bea was the conscience of the group and the unspoken leader of the sistahs. She was retired from her customer training consulting work, although her biggest clients still hired her for special occasions. She was that good. The sistahs tended to give credence to whatever Bea, with her twinkly blue, intelligent eyes and forever-present straw hat, had to say.

"Oh, I'll reschedule," said Dawn, disgusted. "But y'all better be up to date on yours too. If I have to get booby-trapped, so do you."

The sistahs chuckled, and Lola spoke up, "Judith, you did bring gumbo, right? I'm starving. I spent the morning over at the Southern Hotel working on their spring flower beds." Lola was a landscaper who owned Fleur de Lis Landscaping. In addition to the business, she had a law degree which she wielded when needed to the advantage of her sistahs and local political activities in which she engaged. She recently married Bud Broussard for the second time after divorcing years ago because, as she puts it, "I just didn't get enough of that fine man the first time!" Lola's fiery red hair, freckles, smarts, banty rooster-energy, and wicked humor matched her best friend, Dawn, and they often matched wits.

"Of course, I have gumbo," said Judith, walking over to stir the big stainless pot sitting on the heating element in the cafe corner of the gallery. They served coffee and homemade pastries daily alongside the extraordinary art painted by Judith and other local artists. The coffee and food offerings gave the gallery a community feel, and it was often a meeting place for locals. Judith continued, "I made my mom's gumbo recipe, as usual. I was in such a hurry today that I almost let Marty make it, but I knew y'all would kill me if I didn't show up with my mom's recipe."

"I love your mom's gumbo," said Dawn, then added with a grin, "Of course...my mama's gumbo makes your mom's gumbo cry with envy!"

The sistahs all chuckled at this running, competitive joke they used every chance they had. Judith gave the expected, barbed response, "And my mom's gumbo makes your mom's gumbo taste like leftover swill. Or maybe yesterday's dishwater or..."

"Roadkill!" yelled Lola, laughing gleefully.

Dawn laughed, but she shot her friends a dangerous look then grabbed a bowl and shoved it at Judith. "OK, prove it. Put up, or shut up."

Chuckling, Judith took the bowl, ladled out some of the rich, brown concoction loaded with sausage and chicken, and added a scoop of fluffy, white rice in the center. Then she served bowls to the rest of the sistahs and joined them at the cafe tables. They dove in appreciatively. Truthfully, all of the sistahs made excellent gumbo, but they refused to acknowledge that fact. It would spoil their fun. But nothing would spoil their appetites.

Lola broke the silence by asking, "By the way, Judith, how is Marty? We haven't seen him in a while."

"Marty? He's the best. He's still making furniture every day in his shop and selling it at arts and crafts shows on the weekends."

"Is he still trying to get you to marry him?" asked Dawn, and the other sistahs chuckled.

"Oh, he's cooled his jets a bit, thank God! I don't think he believed me for the longest time that I really didn't want to get married again. But I think he's finally getting the message."

"Well, I'm so glad I married Bud again," said Lola and smiled happily at the thought of her big, handsome man she'd married again after many years apart. "In fact, if we broke up again, I'd probably marry him a third time. He's such a good guy."

The sistahs were quiet for a few minutes, which only ever happened when they had fantastic food sitting in front of them. As Judith spooned a heaping spoon of gumbo into her mouth, she savored the rich, melded flavors, and her eyes roved appraisingly around the gallery. The walls were hung with various sizes of her bold, colorful art depicting the groups of women she loved to create. The women in the paintings were much like her friends who supported one another and enjoyed each other's company. Judith had named them the Gumbeaux Sistahs paintings years ago, a name that she had passed onto her real group of friends.

Judith thought about how Bea, Dawn, Lola, Helen, and she were drawn together out of true friendship. Since they had become a group, other women had also joined as honorary Gumbeaux Sistahs. These included Trinity Hebert, Dawn's sister, Bitsy Rogers, Judith's old co-worker from when she worked at the Covington Art Gallery, and a few women who were taking turns sitting on the various Friendship Benches around town. So many women had the heart of true friendship, and Judith felt enormously lucky to know them all and have them involved in her life.

Helen interrupted Judith's thoughts, "I would have shown up anyway for this meal, but you did mention an emergency, Judith. I've got a client I need to get to at one-thirty, so out with it." She winked at Judith as she dug into her gumbo. Helen was a Reiki Master and massage therapist who lived in nearby Mandeville. The sistahs sometimes took advantage of her skillful hands when they needed to unclench or just relax. She also had a thriving business concocting her own essential oil line. When Helen gave an oil workshop, attendees came from all over the south to learn from her. Helen was also the sistah the others went to for nutritional advice. She was knowledgeable in the field and grew much of her own organic vegetables and fruits. Helen stood in their midst, a gentle presence in her long, pastel, comfy skirts she preferred year-round. She was clearly an old hippie. She had recently adopted a teenage son, Cooper, away from an abusive family situation, and neither of them had ever been happier.

"I'm glad you approve of my mom's gumbo, Helen," quipped Judith, then added jokingly, "Say, isn't that like admitting it's the best in town?"

"I would not go that far," said Helen drolly. "But seriously, if you say it's an emergency, then you need our help. And here we are. So, what's up?"

"It's about the Friendship Bench."

"What about it?" Bea encouraged.

"So, you know how occasionally someone will come and sit on the bench and stump us so badly that we don't know how to handle it? Well, I've got a doozy!" said Judith, shaking her head.

"Oh my God, you too?" asked Helen.

"Must be the moon phase or something," said Dawn. "I've got one that is bugging me to death!"

They looked at each other, and Bea spoke up, "Well, we've all agreed to come to each other when we had a visitor that confounded us. Sometimes it doesn't quite seem like they need a therapist, just a good solution. But sometimes it's hard to come up with one on the spot. I know I've had to ask your opinions on bench visitors in the past. We should really confer with each other more often."

Helen agreed and added, "Sometimes, I think if I just give the problem a little more time, I'll come up with a solution. But it just doesn't always work, and I need help."

"I think we're all guilty of not asking for enough help," said Bea thoughtfully.

"I know I am," said Lola and Helen simultaneously. They grinned at each other.

"Well, starting today, whenever we get together, we should take a few minutes to ask if anyone needs a little help with visitors. Does everyone agree?" asked Bea.

"Absolutely," agreed Helen. "We really should. I mean, we already ask permission of everyone who sits on the bench to discuss their problems with the other Gumbeaux Sistahs, and then we don't always do it. By the way, I've never had anyone say no to giving permission, have you?"

The other sistahs shook their heads.

"OK, let's declare it an official Gumbeaux Sistahs rule even though there is no such thing, is there?" laughed Lola.

Dawn answered, laughing, "We should make it a rule that you keep your mouth shut." She made a sassy face at her friend. The two of them could never resist an opportunity to make a friendly dig at each other.

The others joined in the good-natured laughter, and then Judith interrupted, "So, it sounds like each of you have recently encountered a visitor who could have used a good 'putting-our-heads-together.' So, let's start. I'll go first. This woman sat on the bench with me yesterday. Her name is Mrs. Melrose. Maddie Melrose. And she's not from Covington or nearby. She's here from Natchez, Mississippi, visiting her lawyer about a real estate matter. I swear she's got to be about ninety years old, but she's sharper than a tack—and almost as painful to deal with. Let's just say she doesn't suffer fools gladly."

"Oh well, then don't let her near Lola," teased Dawn, throwing her balled-up napkin at her friend.

Lola lobbed the napkin right back at Dawn so that Bea had to chide them, "Calm down, you two. Go on, Judith."

"Well, Mrs. Melrose pulled up in front of the gallery yesterday in her Mercedes and, get this—she has a driver! He got out and opened the door for her."

"Wow," said Dawn, impressed, "I want one of those."

"You don't need a Mercedes," cracked Lola. "You need a semi-truck for all the shopping you do."

"No, not the Mercedes. I want a driver! Can you imagine how convenient that would be?" She adopted a snobby tone and looked down her nose at Lola and said, "Charles, drop me off at Galatoire's and wait for me while I lunch with Trinity.' Good Lord, I hate to admit it, but I sincerely would love that, and can you please get that for me for my next birthday?"

Helen interrupted, "Having a driver these days is like something from another age, unless you're an A-list movie star or something."

"Well, it's not over the top for Mrs. Melrose. Something tells me she's accustomed to old money and quite comfortable with the niceties." Judith went on, "So, anyway, she walks up using a solid gold cane—OK, I'm kidding about the solid gold part—but she plops herself down on the bench in the grandest, most elegant way—as if she owned the place."

"What did she want to talk about?" asked Bea, keeping the conversation on track.

"She started out by telling me how her husband had been a well-respected surgeon in Natchez where they have lived forever. Mrs. Melrose was born there and apparently comes from old family lines—and old money as well. They had no children, but they had a full life, enjoying a high position in Natchez society. The thing is that her husband, Dr. Melrose, died about a year and a half ago. She's spent the time since selling his medical practice and taking care of their other businesses, mostly real-estate based, including owning a building in downtown Covington two blocks from here."

"Losing a spouse is such a hard thing to have to deal with," said Bea, a sudden sadness taking over her usual-happy face. She and her husband had lived in New Orleans until he had a heart attack many years ago.

"Yes, indeed. No matter what the circumstances," agreed Helen, whose abusive husband had died five years earlier.

Dawn, who was more recently widowed looked momentarily stricken. She was inclined to still have bouts of sudden grief when reminded of her husband's passing. They had been happily married for over thirty years and built their accounting business together, enjoying much success and raising their two now-grown children.

All three of these sistahs had scrambled after their husbands' deaths to start new lives and take care of family businesses—or to start new ones.

"My heart goes out to her," said Bea sincerely.

"Well, now she's got all their financials squared away, and guess what? She going on ninety and bored silly. At least that's what she says."

"Hmm. That may be true," agreed Dawn. "But it might also be fear talking. Do you remember when Dan first passed, how I had to just keep busy doing, well, anything, so that I didn't spend all of my time thinking of him? Judith, I barely let you take a turn working in the gallery. I was taking all the shifts I could just to have people to talk to."

"I remember, Dawn. I got a lot of painting done at home for the gallery during that period, but I was so worried about you."

"I'm better now," said Dawn, looking sad. "Of course, I'll never be quite the same, but it's hard to keep a good woman down, right?"

"Yes, it is," answered Lola. "It's too bad we don't know any." Dawn chuckled and reached over gave her best friend a little shove.

Bea interrupted so that their friendly battle would cease for the moment, "So what does Mrs. Melrose want? Does she want to talk about how to keep occupied? Does she need friends? Is she in danger from her grief and depression?"

"Well, that's the thing," explained Judith. "And it was the strangest part. She wouldn't tell me."

"What?" asked Lola. "What do you mean? What did she say?"

"She marched up to the bench, sat down, and told me I needed to sit up straight, to start. Can you imagine? Then she told me her entire family history—how they were from Natchez and lived in a stately old antebellum home in town. She told me all about her husband. And then…she challenged me."

"To a duel?" asked Dawn, shocked.

"Yes, Dawn," answered Judith, rolling her eyes. "We're meeting in the morning under the Dueling Oak in City Park. Can I count on you to be my second? It will be a fight to the death with paint brushes at ten paces."

"Wait, how about using rolling pins?" laughed Helen, who baked all the scones for the gallery cafe.

"How about mascara wands?" said Lola.

"Maybe she'll swing at you with her solid gold cane," added Bea with a grin.

The sistahs were laughing so hard at this point that they couldn't even talk until Bea finally got them back on track again.

"OK, OK," she said, "So, what exactly is this challenge? For real this time."

"Mrs. Melrose told me that she'd heard about the Gumbeaux Sistahs and our Friendship Bench from her attorney in town, and that she has had something very important to discuss with us, but that she needed to discuss it back in her hometown—in Natchez."

"In Natchez?" asked Ellen in surprise. "What did she mean by that?"

"She sort of demanded that *all* of us to come up to Natchez, weekend after next, to talk to her."

"All of us?" asked Lola. "That's weird—and a little pushy, don't you think?"

"Oh, and that's not all," Judith went on. "She's giving me only two days to respond to her request or her offer is off the table."

"Sheesh! Pushier and pushier," said Lola.

"Here's where it gets really mysterious," said Judith. "She said she'd make it worth my while. And also that we'd be staying with her in her mansion. And that's all she said, really. She gave me her number and took off down the street with her driver."

Dawn looked thoughtfully at Lola and then at the others and said, "You know, I don't know about you all, but presuming she's not an axe murderer, this sounds like an adventure to me!"

Lola's eyebrows shot up. "That's true! I've always wanted to visit Natchez, and it might be cool to stay in one of those gorgeous old houses. I'd love to see what the grounds outside look like too," she said, ever the landscaper.

Cautiously the sistahs all turned towards Bea to see what she thought. "Well, can everyone even get away for that weekend?"

The sistahs looked at their phone calendars and found themselves all nodding. Bea grinned and said, "OK, even if Mrs. Melrose turns out to be a crazy axe murderer, I guess we've got ourselves a road trip, sistahs."

"He's lying. He just knew he could get free coffee here."
—Zoe

# CHAPTER 3

J ust as the sistahs were letting out a cheer, Zoe Abadie and Cooper Landry walked into the front door of the gallery. Zoe was Dawn's eighteen-year-old granddaughter who had moved to Covington a year ago and now worked side by side with Lola in her landscaping business. And Cooper was Helen's nineteen-year-old, recently adopted son who was studying art at Loyola University across the lake in New Orleans. After a rocky start in their relationship, during which time the two of them wished curses upon one another, Cooper and Zoe had eventually become careful friends. The sistahs always watched them closely, eyeing each other and raising their brows questioningly whenever the two of them showed up together. They were looking for tell-tale signs as to what type of relationship the two young people had going these days— enemies, just friends, or more.

"Well, look who's here!" said Helen. "What are you two kids up to?" She turned and secretly winked at Dawn.

"We're looking for you all," said Coop with a sly smile and then added with his usual edge of sarcasm, "We just don't get to visit enough, do we?"

"He's lying," said Zoe, laughing. "He just knew he could get free coffee here—and, as luck would have it, some gumbo by the looks of it."

"OK, you got me," admitted Cooper as Judith handed each of them a cup of coffee and started serving up gumbo as well.

"We're always good for coffee here for you, Coop. Did you invite Zoe to come meet you here?" she fished.

"Actually, we just ran into each other outside," said Zoe, reaching for her bowl.

Lola spoke up, "Zoe is here to meet me. We're going to tackle a new backyard garden account."

"That's true, but I admit I like the free coffee too." Zoe grinned at them.

"So, what's new with you two?" asked Bea. "Coop, how's school?"

"It's pretty awesome. I'm learning a lot and meeting some pretty cool people. There are so many talented students in my classes."

"Especially you," interrupted Helen, giving her boy an affectionate pat on his shoulder.

"That goes without saying," he joked. "But seriously, it's inspiring to be around all those artists. We have so much in common, and I think a lot of us worry about the same thing—how we can make a living with our art after graduation."

"Oh, that reminds me," interrupted Lola. "Excuse me, Coop, but talking about art and the Friendship Bench made me think of this. A woman came by the other day, and she's an artist too. She's a little younger than we are, sistahs, so that means she's getting a late start on an art career. She spent her life raising kids, and she had a demanding job too. She managed the local Dollar Store for forever. She still does. And to tell you the truth, when she showed up at the bench, I think she was hoping to run into you, Judith, since you're an artist and own the gallery. She wanted to talk to someone about what Coop just said—making a living at art."

Judith nodded thoughtfully, saying, "It seems as if a lot of people go through their lives with art in their souls or an urge to create, but for some reason or other it gets pushed to the side. Then when they get a little older, it pops up again and demands attention in some form. I guess it's not an urge that can be denied forever."

"It sounds like she has the same concerns that the younger people in your class have, Coop. Does anyone ever talk to y'all about it at school? The teachers, I mean?"

"We talk about it a little, but mostly we talk about art theory and technique," he said with a mouthful. He had moved on from gumbo to one of Helen's croissants that she'd baked for the gallery cafe that morning.

Judith turned to Lola, "So, what did you tell that woman on the bench?"

"I told her that I would talk to you. Is that OK? I think she would benefit from a conversation with you."

"You got her name and number?"

"Sure thing," answered Lola. "Her name is Lisa Langley, and here's her number." She handed Judith a slip of paper.

Helen went back to Cooper, "Do you think they'll get some speakers in there to talk to the students about this subject—making a living at art?"

"I sure hope so," he answered, "I've mentioned it to the head of the department and my main teacher, Mr. Bennett, a couple of times. He's my also my favorite instructor by the way. He's super nice, and it seems like all the girls in class have a crush on him because I guess he's kind of handsome. I think some of the guys in class do too."

"Hmm, maybe I should talk to him," said Dawn. "We know a lot of people in the art business, and maybe we could come up with some help for him."

"Thanks, Aunt Dawn. I'll bet you could come up with something and the students would love that. And I'll bet Mr. Bennett would be all over the idea."

"I'm happy to help you, Coop." Dawn gave him a big hug, and he turned red all the way up to his ears.

"Look at him blush!" said Lola yelled, "Let's get him, sistahs! Group hug!" They mobbed the young man, and he yelped with protest.

"Get in here, Zoe!" teased Helen.

"I think he's got more than he can handle as it is," Zoe said with a wry smile at Cooper. He blushed even more.

"OK, that's enough of torturing Coop," laughed Judith. "So, Lola, I'll call your lady and talk to her soon."

"OK, great. And now Zoe and I should probably get a move on," said Lola.

"Oh no, you don't," said Dawn, standing up. "Since we're using this time to talk about our Friendship Bench challenges, I've got one for you too. And it's a doozy!"

"Well, I'll just wait outside and give you your privacy while you finish up," said Zoe, heading to the door.

"And I'd better hit the road," said Coop and followed her while five pairs of sistah-eyes followed them out. They all grinned knowingly.

"So, I've decided to turn to a life of crime."
—Sissy

# CHAPTER 4

"I'm so glad you brought this up, Judith," began Dawn. "I was going to call y'all about it. I did talk to Lola, but I could use all of your opinions. Especially since it deals with a criminal."

"A what?" asked Helen, horrified. Then she quickly got a mischievous look, "What did you do now, Dawn?"

"Funny, Helen. You sound just like Lola."

"I'm giving her lessons," said Lola.

"Quiet down, please, girls. This sounds serious," interrupted Bea. "What are you talking about, Dawn. What criminal?"

"Well, it's more of a beginner criminal problem rather than a hardened criminal one."

"Tell us," said Judith.

"It's Mrs. Etheridge," said Dawn.

"Mrs. Etheridge?" said Helen, shocked. "That sweet little lady? The one that helps out with the altar flowers at St. John's?"

"I know, right?" said Dawn. "I wouldn't have guessed that about her in a million years. But I think she's serious about it! So, here's what I know. Two days ago, she came and sat on the bench with me. She'd been to the bench before, so I thought we were going to talk again about her only son who moved to Washington State. They don't really talk much anymore, and she misses him. But that's not what happened. Instead, when she started talking, I swear the hair on my arms stood on end."

"What did she say?" asked Helen.

Lola interrupted excitedly, "Wait till y'all hear this! Dawn told me, and it's got me stumped about what to do too."

"So, as I said, she sits down on the bench and tells me that she's feeling old, used up, lonely, and that it feels like her life is over."

"Oh no, the poor thing," said Bea sadly.

"I know. I felt so bad for her at first," answered Dawn. "But then she told me, and I quote, 'So I've decided to turn to a life of crime.'"

Helen's mouth fell open, and Bea let out a gasp of surprise.

Dawn went on, "She told me that she's already 'hit' several local businesses!"

"What did she mean by that?" squeaked Bea, shocked.

"She says she's been going into stores and shoplifting. It seems to be kind of a game to her. I think she's really getting off on it too. She admitted to me that she's given herself a challenge. Each time she 'pulls a caper,' as she calls it, the item she steals has to be bigger than the last one. It started out with a candy bar, but this last time she stole a nice purse from a local store. She wouldn't tell me which store it was, but she had the nerve to bring the darned thing to the bench with her. I'm telling you, she was proud of it!"

"Oh, good Lord!" said Judith. "She's going to end up in jail. And some poor local store owner is out a purse!"

"And God only knows what else she's stolen," said Helen, shaking her head. "Wait, I know. Let's check the crime section of the newspaper to see if there's any mention of local shop thefts."

"Good idea," said Dawn hurried over to the register where the laptop was stored. She flipped it open and yelled out, "What's the darned password again, Judith?" She swore under her breath as she tried several combinations. "I don't know about you ladies, but I don't have any more passwords left in me."

Judith reminded her, and Dawn got on to the local newspaper website. After scrutinizing the reported crimes Dawn said, "Well, I don't see anything, unless she's up to carjacking over in New Orleans at this point."

"Dear Lord! You don't think that will happen, do you?" asked Judith, but Dawn was busy typing. Suddenly she gasped, "Wow! Y'all are not going to believe this."

"What did you find, dear?" asked Bea.

Dawn leaned closer to the computer and said, "There's this article here all about how elder crime is on the rise—as much as 44% in some places it says!" She read on, "The article said that much of the rise can be attributed to the aging general population, but much of it is due to loneliness and boredom in seniors. Poverty can play a role too."

"Is Mrs. Etheridge impoverished?" asked Helen.

"I think she's struggling," said Dawn, nodding. "She mentioned that her Social Security is barely covering the rising cost of food these days."

"That's probably true of so many seniors," said Bea. "How frightening that must be for them."

Dawn added, "She's pretty lonely too since her son left for Washington and I have the feeling it's more about this issue than anything." She looked up from the computer at the sistahs. "I'll tell you something else too. Mrs. Etheridge hinted that she was planning something bigger. I think she's out of control." She shook her head, alarmed.

"This is serious," murmured Bea.

Lola piped up, "So what do we do? Should we call the police?"

"Oh no! I hope we don't have to go that far," said Helen. "I hate the idea of the police dragging poor Mrs. Etheridge off to jail!"

"Maybe a good talking to would bring her to her senses," suggested Bea. "Maybe being firm and telling her like it is would help."

"With a threat thrown in for good measure," nodded Lola, narrowing her eyes.

"Well, look," said Dawn, rejoining the sistahs at the table. "She's coming back to the bench to talk on Wednesday, and that's my shift again. Let me try talking to her one more time, and we'll see what happens. And I'll keep y'all posted."

"Maybe that's the best we can do today," agreed Bea. "But let's meet again about this soon, just in case."

"Let's hope she doesn't get in trouble before then," said Lola, rolling her eyes.

Zoe didn't know whether to smile or throw
a rock at his head.

# CHAPTER 5

After Zoe and Cooper stepped outside and stood on the sidewalk in front of the Gumbeaux Sistahs Gallery, Zoe said, "Lola and I have a big landscaping job today. We should be working it all week." Then she turned to Cooper, "Don't you have class today?"

"I do this afternoon. It's Mr. Bennett's class, actually, so it's a good one. I'd better get going," said Coop, fishing keys out of his pocket.

Zoe reached out and held onto his sleeve saying, "Hey before you go, I need to ask you something."

"What's that?" he asked, thinking she might be going to ask for help with her computer or something tech related. He was the one all the sistahs went to with computer troubles.

Instead, Zoe said, "You need to come with my Grandma Dawn and me to the Chef's Soiree event on Saturday night."

Cooper couldn't hide his surprise and asked, smiling, "Really? Wait—I *need* to come with you?" He laughed, and then asked suddenly, "Hey, that means free food, doesn't it?"

"Yes, the food will no doubt be fantastic, and Grandma Dawn has free tickets." She looked a bit embarrassed, and Coop narrowed his eyes at her.

"Wait a minute. Are you asking me on a date?" He looked like he might start teasing, so she said quickly, "Are you crazy? Of course not! I just know you like free food, is all. Can't a person do something nice for you?"

He was grinning broadly now and jumped in to tease her with both feet, "I knew it! You're in love with me, aren't you, Zoe Abadie?"

"You are such an ass, Coop." She was getting angry now and said, "Forget I said anything."

"Oh no. No takebacks. It's a date, and you and I and your grandma are stepping out this Saturday. I will wine and dine you—all for free, of course. No, I accept your request for a date, and I'll see you on Saturday." He was grinning as he walked away from her backwards down the street.

Zoe didn't know whether to smile or throw a rock at his head.

"Weddings can be wonderful, but they can be minefields too."
—Bea

# CHAPTER 6

Bea stayed behind with Judith when the Gumbeaux Sistahs finished lunch and left for their jobs and errands.

"Let me help you finish putting things away, Judith, while I wait for my next Friendship Bench visitor. I've got a few minutes to kill till my shift starts."

"Great, thanks," said Judith. "Could you just push the chairs in to the tables, and then we're done. I'm just going to put this gumbo pot in my car, and then I've got to get started on this month's bookkeeping. Ugh. My favorite job, it is not."

Bea chuckled, "I know, it's a necessary evil. I used to hate it too, but it was always so satisfying to see how a business looks on paper, especially if it's a good month."

"Well, it was, thank the Lord," said Judith. "Art sales are always pretty good for the gallery, but the cafe has been a surprise success. It really adds to the bottom line." She looked up, glancing out of the front windows. "Speaking of which, it looks like a couple of our cafe regulars are here now."

When the front doorbell tinkled, Judith called out, "Good morning," to the customers. Bea waived goodbye and let Judith wait on her customers. She walked out the front door, took her spot on the Friendship Bench, and waited for her first visitor of the day to arrive.

She didn't have to wait long before a woman in a grey pantsuit and silver-shot brown hair walked slowly up the street. Her face was pale, and her shoulders stooped. *Unhappy,* Bea thought, as the woman neared the bench. But when she was close enough to see, Bea was stricken by the sheer amount of sadness in the woman's demeanor.

Bea didn't recognize her from around town, but she recognized that deep pain reflected in her eyes. The same type of pain had been in Bea's eyes once upon a time after she'd lost her husband to a heart attack. Bea felt horrified at the sight of the suffering caused by a deep loss. She knew that although she didn't feel it as deeply now after so many years, it wasn't buried too far beneath the surface. It momentarily shocked her. That pain had almost cost Bea her own life, and she quickly took stock of her emotions and her strength levels. She felt reassured, took a deep breath, and plastered a smile across her face as she welcomed the woman to the bench with as much warmth as she could muster.

"Hi, I'm Bonnie Phillips," said the woman softly as she sat down.

"Hello, dear. I'm Bea Walker" she said, taking the woman's hand and holding it inside both of her own for a moment. Bea believed in the power of human touch and in that moment, she tried to convey some reassurance. "Welcome to the Friendship Bench. Is this your first visit to the bench?"

"Yes, it is," said Bonnie. "I'm really not even sure what I'm doing here."

"Well," said Bea, "It's been my experience that people who show up here usually have a good reason for doing so."

The woman was quiet for a moment, looking at her hands. The she spoke in a hush, "I didn't mean—being here on the bench. I don't know what I'm doing here, in this world, in this life. That's the problem." She looked directly at Bea. "And it's a problem I may have to solve very soon."

Her words chilled Bea to the bone. She felt dark clouds closing in on the two of them.

"Bonnie," Bea said softly. "Please tell me what's going on. Take your time. We have as long as you need."

"Nothing," said the other woman. "Absolutely nothing."

Bea tried draw her out by asking questions. She needed to get Bonnie's story if she was going to try and help. She began with, "Do you live nearby?"

"I live in Mandeville," she responded. Bea nodded. Mandeville was a picturesque little city about twenty minutes away from downtown Covington.

"Do you have family there?" asked Bea. "Who do you live with?"

"I've been divorced for many years, so I only live with my little dog, Huffy. She's a little dachshund."

"Oh, those are wonderful dogs," said Bea encouragingly.

"She's a sweet old girl."

"Do you have any children?"

"Yes. I have a daughter. Her name is Jenny Matheson, and she lives up in Baton Rouge with her husband Matt and my granddaughter, Jilly, who is five."

"Oh, that's lovely, dear. Do you get to see them often?"

Bonnie clenched her jaw and blurted out, "Never." Bea was taken aback at the bluntness. Then she noticed tears spring into Bonnie's eyes. "I never see them. I've never even met little Jilly."

Bea breathed in sharply. There was so much pain in the woman's life, and Bea could feel it more every minute that passed. "That's a terrible shame, Bonnie. Is it too hard for each of you to make the trip?"

"Not harder than any other hour-and-a-half trip, I imagine," said Bonnie. "But neither of us will ever be making that trip." Anger flashed in Bonnie's eyes, and Bea took it as a warning.

Bea was quiet for a while then said, "It sounds as if you and your daughter have had some sort of falling out."

Bonnie nodded miserably.

"How long ago did that happen, dear?"

Bonnie thought a moment. "It's been seven years," she said, nodding.

Bea reached for the woman's hand and touched it sympathetically with her own. "That's long time."

Bonnie nodded and shrugged, looking at the sidewalk.

"Do you want to talk about it, dear?" asked Bea, carefully.

"No, not really," said Bonnie. Then she added suddenly, "It's all so stupid. It's actually embarrassing."

"Boy, I know that one," agreed Bea. "Listen, we all do stupid things, believe me."

"Well, this one could win a statewide stupid contest," said Bonnie, shaking her head. "It was all over her wedding."

"Ah," said Bea knowingly. "Weddings are wonderful, but they can be minefields too. Every time one of my friends tells me their daughter or son or grandchild is getting married, I can't help but advise them to be extra patient and forgiving during that time. People can say and do hurtful things when planning for their big day. I call it Wedding Fatigue." She went on, "And I've heard some stories, let me tell you. Weddings make people crazy. I mean, I love weddings. They can be such beautiful celebrations, but people can get mental about them really fast. As I said, I advise people to tread lightly around wedding preparations and keep your patience at the ready."

"That's good advice, Bea. I wish my daughter and I had heard it before she got married."

"Why don't you tell me about it, dear?" asked Bea encouragingly.

"Well, as I said, it was really stupid. And shocking too the way the whole thing got out of control. So, here's what happened. I'm divorced from Jenny's father, and then he died a couple of years before the wedding. Jenny's father was the major breadwinner when we were married, and after the divorce I had to scrounge to make a living. I never had a lot of money, and I knew I couldn't afford the wedding. But my son-in-law's parents are wealthy as can be and offered to pay for the whole shebang."

Bea nodded and Bonnie went on, "All that was great, and I was so happy for my daughter that his parents could afford it, and she could have a lovely wedding. Then the groom's parents held an engagement at their beautiful home, and of course I went. But I'm afraid I didn't exactly have a good time. His family basically ignored me all night, shuffled me off to the side with some strangers, and hung out together the entire evening. No one even offered me a beverage, for heaven's sake."

"Oh no," sympathized Bea.

"I was so uncomfortable and so embarrassed. The only people I knew were my daughter and her future husband, Matt, but they stayed with his family the whole night. I couldn't believe how my daughter was treating me. I mean, I tried to mingle, but it was hard. I'd come to the party to celebrate with my daughter, and everyone acted like I didn't belong there."

"Oh, that's not right," said Bea shaking her head.

"So, I ended up leaving a bit early. To tell you the truth, I couldn't wait to get out of there, but I stayed for what I thought was a decent amount of time."

"Go on," encouraged Bea.

"The next day, my daughter called and asked why I was so rude and why I left early. You can imagine my surprise. So, I was honest with her. I told her what I had experienced. Honestly, I fully expected that, once she had heard me out, she would show some understanding. Maybe even apologize. But the way she saw it was that I came to the party, stayed by myself in a corner, and hardly spoke to anyone. Her fiancé's mother even said something nasty about me to her. I tell you, I was shocked that my daughter had turned on me so strongly about the whole thing, and that she wouldn't see my side of the story."

"Oh dear," said Bea.

"Of course, then I ended up getting upset with her, and she with me, and we had words. To tell you the truth, even then I expected that a couple of days would go by and then we'd make up."

"That's not what happened, I take it?"

"It sure wasn't. What happened was that Jenny mentioned what I'd said to her fiancé, and did it stop there? No ma'am! It did not. Matt went and told his parents that I said they were rude."

"Oh boy," said Bea.

"Oh boy is right. So, the next thing I know, Matt's mother was calling me and got real uppity. She said, how dare I call her rude when she had invited me into her home and was paying for the whole wedding on top of it.'"

Bea's wrung her hands together, dreading to hear what was next. "What did you do?"

"I'm afraid I wasn't very cool, Bea. I was so hurt and felt so put upon that I lost my temper and called her an entitled, ignorant snob."

Bea slapped her hand to her forehead, "You didn't!"

"I did, in fact. Then she called me an ungrateful, low-class idiot."

"Oh no," said Bea mournfully.

"And then it went downhill from there."

"What?" winced Bea. "How could it get worse?"

Bonnie looked down at her hands and her eyes welled up. "It just did. It got much worse. Matt's mother uninvited me to the wedding."

Bea heaved a sigh, "Oh boy."

"And the worst part of it is that my daughter basically backed her up. She sent me a text—a text mind you! It said, 'You need to stop making trouble. I'm trying to marry into this family, and a lot of damage has already been done.'"

"Oh, dear. That had to hurt."

"It did."

"So, what happened?"

"Well, the day of the wedding came, and I put on my new pearl grey, mother-of-the-bride dress that I paid good money for, and I went to that wedding. There was no way in hell that I wasn't going to see my daughter get married."

"Good for you, Bonnie."

"I sat in the back of the church though. I know that Matt's mother saw me at the wedding. She gave me such a hateful look. But I didn't care about that. The important thing was that I saw my beautiful daughter walk down the aisle. I don't think she saw me, but that was okay. I did what I came to do. I'm her mother, and I belonged there. Of course, I didn't go to the reception. I didn't need to. I saw what I needed to."

"Of course you did," said Bea.

"But Bea, it never ended. Never." Now the tears really did come. "I've texted and emailed my daughter, but she has never replied to me. They live in Baton Rouge, so it's not very far. But she's never invited me to her new home. Not even when she was pregnant and had her little girl, my granddaughter. She did have the decency to send me a birth announcement in the mail, but that was it. I sent her a nice baby gift, hoping that it would help matters, but it didn't. I feel like his family has brain-washed her into thinking that she had a new family, and that was all she needed. That she doesn't need her mother anymore. But she does, Bea. I could be helping her out with my granddaughter all this time. She thinks she doesn't need me. And Bea, even if she doesn't, I need her."

Her tears fell gently from the saddest eyes Bea had ever seen. She felt her heart cracking wide open for the woman.

"That's so sad, Bonnie," said Bea softly. Then she added in a determined tone, "But you can't give up."

The woman raised her head slowly and looked at Bea's kind face, "I think I have given up."

The softness of her voice and the deep depths of sorrow in Bonnie's eyes gave Bea chills. "What do you mean, Bonnie?"

"Nothing," the woman said in a hushed voice.

"Bonnie, are you in trouble?"

"You could probably say that," she muttered.

"You can talk to me, you know. I'm safe as houses. And I'll be honest with you. After my husband died years ago, I was in pretty rough shape and didn't know which way to turn. If it wasn't for the fact that a friend gave me a chance to say how I was feeling, well… I'm not sure what would have happened."

Bonnie was watching her with interest, so Bea went on, "What I'm saying is, maybe I'm your chance too. I'd like to help you. Can you tell me what you're thinking?"

Bonnie looked down at her hands as she twisted her fingers back and forth nervously. Bea could barely hear her whisper, "I just don't see the point anymore."

With her heart hurting for this woman, Bea put her hand over Bonnie's and asked carefully, "You're not thinking of hurting yourself, are you?"

"I wouldn't call it hurting myself, Bea. I would call it ending the hurt."

Bea sighed and pushed gently for Bonnie to continue, "What were you thinking of doing, Bonnie?"

Bonnie hesitated and whispered, "I'm not sure yet, Bea." Then she went on boldly, "I've thought of pills, or even jumping off a building. Sometimes, I look at the beams in my garage ceiling and picture myself hanging there."

"Oh my God, Bonnie!," said Bea, horrified. A thought occurred to her, "Tell me this, is there a gun in your house?"

"Well, no—I don't have one of those."

As terrible as the situation was, Bea was slightly relieved to hear that. It's one of the first things the police would ask if they were questioning Bonnie. If the woman was telling the truth, then perhaps there was a small hope. A gun made things like this all that much easier plus it could pose a threat to anyone who might try and rescue the situation.

Bea pressed on, "Here's something to consider. Don't you think your daughter would suffer terribly from losing you?"

"To tell you the truth, I get the feeling that she wouldn't care one bit. I think she's numb to her feelings for me. Shoot, I'm more worried about my dog missing me than I am about my daughter. I can't see her shedding a single tear."

"I'm sure you're wrong about that. People just don't work that way. She lives in Baton Rouge, you say? You two need to sit down and talk this out. Have you tried just showing up and going to see her?"

"No, I haven't. She won't answer my texts. I don't even dare call. I can just imagine what it would be like in person."

"Tell me about your dog, Huffy. How old is she?"

"She's nine and such a good girl. I've had her since she was a pup. She is the only thing I can count on these days."

"I get that. Dogs are wonderful companions. So, Bonnie, how can you even think about leaving her behind?"

At this Bonnie took a raspy breath, and tears flowed down her face. Bea, ever ready, handed her some tissues that she always kept handy on the bench.

"Thank you," said Bonnie, trying to get control again.

After a moment, Bea asked, "Can I tell you what I think?"

"Might as well," answered Bonnie, her face tear stained.

"I think you're not ready to do anything dramatic. And there's no need to."

Bonnie looked at her briefly, but in that glimpse, Bea saw a touch of interest. "Tell you what, how about you give me a chance to prove that to you?"

"Prove it how?"

"Let me help show you a new side of life—a good side—and what you'd be missing. We're all made up of these chunks of life experience. I think that there are chunks that have been cut out of your life, and those are the very chunks that keep us going." She waited to see Bonnie's reaction and saw a small spark in her eyes.

"You know, I can feel that—chunks missing, as you said," said Bonnie. "I'm not sure I like being referred to as 'chunky' though," Bonnie gave a tiny smile, and Bea's heart lifted with hope.

"OK, first things first. I'm giving you my phone number and also the number of the Suicide Prevention Hotline. Don't argue with me on that last part—it's for just in case. I'll need your phone please." She held out her hand.

Bonnie slowly handed over her phone, and Bea put the numbers in for her. "Also, I'm going to give you the number of someone we are going to call right now, together, because you need to talk to a professional. I can be a friend, but not a professional. Her name is Dr. Janet Forman. I've sent many people to talk to her, and I've been to see her myself. She's great to talk to, and she's smart as a whip. She can help you, Bonnie, if you let her. Are you willing to try?"

Bonnie rolled her eyes and shook her head at Bea. But then she sighed and said, "Oh, very well. I'd be willing to talk to her."

"One more thing, and I'm asking you to trust me one this, you say you have no one you can count on, but that's not true. You can count on me."

Bonnie looked up and nodded thoughfully.

"OK, I'm dialing Dr. Forman's number right now." Bea dialed and spoke to the doctor. Then she introduced Bonnie and put her on the phone. Bonnie made an appointment for the very next day.

After Bonnie hung up, Bea nodded in satisfaction, "That's a very good thing you just did. You won't be sorry." She went on, "Now, let me ask you this. I've got some ideas for you, but first I need your permission on something. The other Gumbeaux Sistahs who are in charge of this Friendship Bench and I often brainstorm and kick around ideas about people who have asked for our help. Sometimes five heads are better than one. I don't have to go into tremendous detail with them, but I'd like to discuss your challenges with them. And I'll tell you, those women are so creative and intuitive. I bet they can help. What do you think of that?"

Bonnie thought for a moment and then said, "I don't mind if you talk things over with them." She paused a moment and looked at Bea with envy, "You're so lucky to have friends like that. What a difference that must make."

Bea looked at the crestfallen expression on Bonnie's face and took note. "OK then," she said. "I may just do that. And there's one more thing."

"What's that?" asked Bonnie.

"How about coming to church with me tomorrow morning? You need company, and God is the best company I know. Besides, I need a coffee buddy afterwards. I'll come by and get you at seven-thirty. Is that alright?"

Bonnie laughed and said, "Are you always this pushy?"

"Oh, you have no idea," grinned Bea.

**"I saw him first!"**
**—Dawn**

# CHAPTER 7

awn sat in her car outside of her sister, Trinity Hebert's, business, the Royal Street Gallery in the French Quarter. She was on her phone, holding for Chuck Bennett, one of Cooper's art teachers at Loyola University. When he came to the phone, she said, "Mr. Bennett? This is Dawn Berard. And I'm about to do you a big favor."

"Hey," he said, laughing. "I like the sound of that, but being a cautious man, can you please tell me a bit more?"

"Of course," said Dawn, business-like. "You don't know me, but I am partners with artist Judith Lafferty in a gallery in Covington. It's called The Gumbeaux Sistahs Gallery.

"Oh yes. I've been across the lake, and I've actually been in your gallery. Judith Lafferty's work is wonderful."

"I'm happy you think so," said Dawn. "It makes this easier."

"OK," he said warmly. "Tell me what I can do for you, Miss Berard."

"Just call me Dawn. OK to call you Chuck?"

"Of course," he answered.

Dawn went on, "I am also best friends with Helen Hoffmann, who is the legal guardian of Cooper Landry in your class."

"Oh yes," he answered. "Cooper's one of my favorite students, actually. He's a rowdy kid with a smart mouth and big talent."

"Yes, that's Coop, alright," smiled Dawn. "He's talented, and he speaks very highly of you and your class. And that's what I want to talk to you about. You see, I was talking to Judith and Coop about art school. They both agreed that while they learned so much in class about art and art techniques, they felt that they were not being prepared for the actual business of being an artist."

"Well, I have to agree there. Artists often think that their work alone will let them make their way into the world. In fact, it very rarely does. I've told the Dean that art students need to have a business background, but I'm afraid this has fallen on some hard-of-hearing ears. I'm sure budgets have a great deal to do with it. On occasion, I've been able to bring in a guest speaker to talk about the life of an artist—about how often it means working at a second job to support your art."

"Exactly," said Dawn triumphantly. "Well, let me tell you, I've got the perfect speaker for you. Judith Lafferty would be happy to come and speak to your class about making a living as an artist if you'd like. I know Coop would like it. He's already told me as much. Do you think you might be interested?"

"That would be wonderful," said Chuck, enthusiastically.

"Terrific, why don't I just come on over to the school, and we'll work out the details? I could be there in fifteen minutes."

"Now? Well, uh, sure that works. Come on over. I'm in the Monroe Hall building."

"I'll find it. See you soon!" said Dawn hurriedly and hung up. She jumped out of her car and ran inside of Trinity's gallery, calling out, "Trinity, where are you?"

Trinity's head popped up from behind a counter where she had been straightening up some shipping supplies. "Good gravy, Dawn! Where's the fire?"

Trinity was a large woman like her sister, newly divorced, and was known as the fashion plate of the sistahs. She was also a New Orleans socialite in her own right. If there was a committee luncheon or a party of Who's Who anywhere in the city, you could bet on Trinity not only being there, but helping to organize the event as well. And when it came to Mardi Gras parties and costumes, Trinity was, hands-down, the queen. She even had a whole room in her apartment above the gallery that was dedicated to the art of costuming. It was chock-full of wigs, boas, sparkly dresses, makeup, and hats. The Gumbeaux Sistahs had been known to raid its contents on special occasions.

Trinity stood up to her full height and straightened her navy-blue tunic over the matching silk crepe pants and pearl necklace. Her shoes matched perfectly, her brown hair was coiffed and highlighted, and her makeup was expert level. She was truly a fashionista.

"Trin," said Dawn hurriedly. "Do you have help in your gallery today? Is anybody here with you?"

"Melba is working today. She's in the back room cleaning up stock back there. We're always fighting dust around here. It's a gallery's enemy, as you well know. I'm lucky she can work a couple of days a week. I can't really afford more than that right now. Going from being married into that oil family, and then divorced and struggling once again takes a bit of getting used to." Trinity's ex-husband, Harry, was one of the Herbert family who owned the River Oil Company. A pre-nup and a divorce put her back to being dependent on her gallery's income, which was decent, but it wasn't oil. She was adjusting accordingly.

"I'm sorry, Trin," said Dawn. "If you need anything, you'll let me know, right?"

"Oh, don't worry about me. I always land on my feet. And Dawn, listen to me and promise me something."

"Sure, what?"

"If I ever talk about getting married again, you will fill my mouth up with Tabasco sauce."

Dawn laughed and hugged her sister, "I can't promise that, but I'll watch out for you, for sure. But never say never."

"I'm saying it, dammit. Never, never, never! This divorce has been so much trouble. I'm swearing off men. I wish I were gay sometimes. Unfortunately, I don't like women that way. But I can't stand men. So, there's just no winning."

Dawn was grinning. "Well, look, let me take your mind off this for the moment. Come take a ride with me. I've got an errand to run, and I'd like your company."

Trinity looked around at the work that needed to be done and made a decision. She called out loudly, "Melba, can you watch the place for a little while?"

Ten minutes later, she and Dawn were in the car heading down St. Charles Avenue, passing the most glorious old mansions and gardens in the city. As they pulled into the Loyola University parking lot, Trinity, who had been listening to Dawn explain their mission said, "So your plan is for Judith to talk to the art class. But you're also planning to bring Lisa Langley, that artist, to hear it? Well, that's a good idea. You told Judith you're doing this, right? I mean, I know she mentioned it, but it sounded to me that she wasn't going to do it right away. And you told Coop, right? And Lisa? You told Lola, right? Lisa is Lola's visitor on the bench—she should be told. Tell me you told them all, Dawn."

"First things first. I need to clear it with Mr. Bennett first. Then I'll take care of everything else."

"OK, I get that, but why am I here?"

"You're here because you're going with me to Creole Creamery afterwards. I've been dreaming of their Creole cream cheese ice cream for like a week now. Doesn't that sound good? And—you're welcome!"

"You know me too well, Dawn."

They parked and walked into the Art Department building and asked for Mr. Bennett. They were directed down the hall, and they walked into what appeared to be an empty classroom. They suddenly spotted a man standing at the front of the class with his back to them. He turned after a moment when he heard them.

Both sisters stopped dead in their tracks and stared. Looking back at them was the most handsome, silver-haired, crystal blue-eyed man either of them had ever seen. Trinity gasped, then whispered to Dawn, "Oh hell! I'm in trouble now!"

Dawn glanced from Mr. Bennett and back to Trinity. Inspiration struck, and she whispered out of the corner of her mouth, "I saw him first."

And the gauntlet had been tossed.

"I just need to stop drinking coffee...when pigs fly."
—Helen

# CHAPTER 8

At that same moment back at the Gumbeaux Sistahs Gallery, Helen pulled up in front of the building and jumped out. Her long, purple skirt and loose, peasant-style blouse swished as she walked up to the front door. She stuck her head inside and yelled, "Who's here?"

Judith pushed her head out from behind the cafe counter and laughed, "Over here, girl. What are you up to?"

"I'm supposed to start my Friendship Bench shift in two minutes, but I just thought I'd say hi. Everything good with you?"

"Yep. Just thinking of our trip to Natchez coming up to visit Mrs. Melrose. You're still going, aren't you?"

"I am indeed," said Helen. "I've always wanted to visit Natchez. I hear it's a real pretty little town with a lot of history behind it."

"Me too," said Judith, wiping her hands from refreshing the coffee pot. "Hey, when you finish up on the bench, stop back in and we'll chat and eat all the cookies."

Helen laughed, "You're on." She ducked back out and took her place on the bench, waiting for her first visitor.

A woman turned the corner and hesitantly walked up the sidewalk towards the gallery. She seemed to be dragging her feet, stopping often to look into store windows along the way. When she finally reached the bench, she asked, "Is it OK to sit?"

"You bet," said Helen with a friendly smile. "I'm Helen Hoffmann, and I'll be your server today," she joked and handed her a business card.

The woman settled in, getting comfortable on the bench, "I'm Dolores Benedict. It's nice to meet you." She folded her arms but not before Helen noticed that there was a perceptible tremor in both hands.

"So, Dolores," began Helen. "How are you doing today?"

"I'm doing just fine," said Dolores firmly, and she pulled her arms in tighter, defiantly.

"Well, OK," said Helen warily. "You know, I don't know you at all, but it feels like something's going on with you. Do you want to tell me about it?"

"No, I don't," said Dolores, but she looked up, and Helen could see a touch of fear in the woman's eyes.

Helen leaned forward, "Dolores, I'll be honest with you. People don't usually come to the bench unless they need to talk about something, or something is going on in their lives that affects them strongly. I want you to know that you're in a safe space here. We talk to all kinds of people about all sorts of things. So, why don't we just cut to the chase, and you tell me what's gotten you upset."

Dolores blurted out, "My children think I have Parkinson's disease."

"Oh dear," said Helen. She asked carefully, "Why do they think that?"

"My hands shake sometimes,"

Helen thought a moment, "Dolores, *do* you have Parkinson's?

"Of course not," said the woman indignantly. "I don't shake any more than you or anyone else does." She paused then added, "What I have is a caffeine problem. Too much coffee makes me nervous."

"How much coffee do you drink a day?" asked Helen, concerned.

"I have one cup in the morning. I know that's not that much, but I think I'm extra sensitive to it. I'd quit, but I love my morning coffee. I don't have many vices to enjoy at my age." She rubbed her hands together nervously, and Helen noticed the tremors once more.

"You know," said Helen, "I've heard that there's a lot of things besides coffee that can make your hands shake—like low blood sugar, anxiety, and some medications. Even lack of sleep can do it. What does your doctor say?"

Dolores looked at her feet and then looked up with a belligerent glare, "I haven't been to see one. And why should I? I just need to stop drinking coffee. But as I said—when pigs fly."

Helen considered the woman for a moment. Choosing her words carefully, she decided to ask some direct questions. "Do you work, Dolores?"

"Yes. I work part-time as a cashier at Rouses supermarket. I've cut down to only two days a week now."

"Are you semi-retired?"

"No," Dolores mumbled. "Just having a hard time working."

"Because of the hand tremors?"

Dolores didn't answer. Helen went on, "So, you're a cashier and not a doctor, right?

The woman looked up at Helen with a puzzled look which turned into a hard, suspicious glint in her eyes, but said nothing still.

Helen pushed forward, "Look, you know what you have to do. Also, I know how crazy-scary this must be for you."

"How would you know?" asked Dolores with scorn.

"Believe me. I've been through some scary stuff too," said Helen softly. "But you're not a doctor, and neither am I. The truth is that it might turn out to be something less frightening than Parkinson's. And instead of finding out, you're choosing to put yourself and your kids through hell by not knowing."

To Helen's great relief, Dolores sighed then nodded. Helen went on, "Do you have someone to go to the doctor with you?"

"I don't want my children to go," huffed Dolores. "They'll just try and tell me what to do. And it's *my* life, for crying out loud."

Helen nodded, "OK, that's easy to fix. I'll come with you."

Dolores looked up, surprised. She looked and Helen with a wary expression, considering. After a moment she said, "Would you really?"

"Yes, I would. In fact, it's no trouble at all."

The woman rubbed her arms as if she were suddenly cold. When she looked up at Helen again, there was a tear in her eye. She spoke softly, "I would like that very much."

Helen smiled and reached out to comfort the woman, "OK, we'll get it done then. You make an appointment this afternoon, and I'll drive you. Give me your address and phone number."

The woman took out a piece of paper and pen and scribbled out her information. Helen promised to call her later in the day and get the appointment time, and the two made their goodbyes. Helen watched Dolores go, and with a sigh, she rose and walked slowly to the front door of the gallery. As she reached for the doorknob she looked down and took note of her own shaking hands.

"That just won't do, love."
—Mrs. Melrose

# CHAPTER 9

"Hello, Judith? This is Mrs. Melrose up in Natchez. How are you, dearest?"

"Oh, hello, Mrs. Melrose. I'm well, thank you. How are things in Natchez?"

"We're fine, just fine. I'm calling to make sure you and your friends are coming weekend after next?"

"Well, I'm not positive yet. I need to solidify plans and…"

Mrs. Melrose interrupted calmly, "That just won't do, love,"

Judith was stunned for a moment and then laughed remembering how wealthy and privileged the older woman seemed to be. She even had her own driver, for Pete's sake. She thought, "She's probably used to getting what she wants." Judith decided to humor her. "I feel pretty certain that everyone is coming. I was going to check with all the sistahs one more time today."

"That's better, dearest. My housekeeper will have everything ready for you when you come."

"What time will you expect us that day?" asked Judith.

"Come at noon, and I'll have lunch ready for you."

"Oh my, you don't have to do all that, Mrs. Melrose."

"It's nothing at all. It's just what we do here. Just get here on time. Twelve, sharp. Don't be late." the woman said sternly. Judith couldn't help but chuckle to herself and think, "*Oh my gravy—she's a tough old bird.*"

"OK then," said Judith. "We'll see you then."

"Yes, you will, dearest. And I have a little surprise for you when you get here," she said and hung up.

Judith stared at her phone a moment, rolling her eyes. She said out loud, "Oh boy. What are we getting ourselves into?"

"Cooper only uses that 'Auntie Judith' stuff when it's going to cost me money—or my sanity."
—Judith

# CHAPTER 10

The next morning Judith drove to the gallery and was surprised to find Dawn, Lola, Cooper, and Trinity there, huddled over the coffee maker.

"We called Bea and Helen, and they are on their way," said Dawn, handing Judith a mug of fresh, hot coffee.

"Did I miss something?" asked Judith, with a puzzled look around, "Did we call a meeting?"

"Not officially," said Lola. "But the four of us wanted to talk to you, and knew you'd be at the gallery. And since we were all getting together, we thought we might as well let Bea and Helen in on the news."

"What news?" asked Bea, pushing her way through the front door. She turned and said to Helen behind her, "They have news, dear."

"Let me get my coffee, and then I want to hear everything," called out Helen.

As coffee was handed out, Judith said, "Ok, spill the beans. I can't imagine what you four want to talk about. And knowing Dawn, I have to admit, I'm a little afraid." She laughed and gave Dawn a nudge with her elbow.

Dawn didn't hesitate, "We have an opportunity for you, partner."

"That's right," said Trinity. "And you just have to do it!"

"Uh oh," said Judith, "Do what, exactly?"

Cooper chimed in, "Please, Auntie Judith."

"Oh boy. Now I know I'm in trouble," Judith said with a chuckle. "Cooper only uses that 'Auntie Judith' stuff when it's going to cost me money—or my sanity."

"Let's just hear them out, dear," encouraged Bea.

"Yes, listen to Bea. Hear us out," said Lola, grinning.

"Alright," said Dawn. "I'll be honest. We need your help on something, and we kind of signed you up for it already anyway." She ducked and waited for Judith's reaction.

Judith's mouth fell open. "You'd better start talking fast, partner. Signed me up for what exactly?"

"Coop needs your help. His whole art department needs you," said Trinity. "And it's the least you could do."

Dawn interrupted Trinity's guilt tactic, "Here's the deal. In the spirit of educating our youth, Coop's art class finds itself in need. They are lacking the advice at school of a seasoned artist who can help them with the business side of making a living through their art. I mean, they have plenty of amazing instruction in art technique and all that, but let's face it, not even their instructors make a living from only creating art. Thank goodness, or we'd have no fabulous teachers, but there's that hole that remains in their instruction."

"That's right," said Cooper. "I've noticed it, and so have the other students."

"So, we thought of you and how you do such an amazing job at the gallery selling your incredible art. You're a genius at it," said Dawn, watching to see if her compliments were hitting their target.

"That's laying it on a bit thick, don't you think? Even for you," said Judith drolly.

"The truth of it is—you are needed, sistah," said Lola firmly.

Judith glanced at Bea who shrugged as if to say, "*They have a point, dear*"

Dawn went on, "Yes, Coop needs you. The students need you. Lola needs you, and Trinity and I need you too."

"Wait, why does Lola need me? And Trinity and you? Where do you two come in?"

Lola spoke up first, "I need you because the subject you will be teaching is the exact one that my Friendship Bench visitor, Lisa, needs to learn. She's an artist who has no idea how to make a living at her art. It's perfect for her."

Judith could see how she might be able to help Lisa. "That's actually good thinking, Lola. I could help Coop and Lisa at the same time. But Dawn and Trinity?"

"I'll let you tell her," smirked Lola.

Trinity jumped in, "Dawn actually doesn't need you, but I do." She shot a dangerous look at her sister.

"I spoke to him first," said Dawn. "And I saw him first too."

"Dawn, what are you, five? Lots of people have seen the man." Trinity shook her finger at her sister. "It doesn't mean that they own him though."

Helen, who had been watching and sipping her coffee, interrupted, "Wait a minute. It's hard to keep up here. Who is *he*?"

"It's Mr. Bennett, my art teacher," said Cooper, rolling his eyes.

"Oh, I see," said Bea and added with a little smile, "Tell me, dears. I don't suppose this Mr. Bennett is good looking, is he?"

Trinity blushed, nodding, and Dawn grinned widely, "Oh man, is he!"

The sistahs hooted with laughter.

"OK, I've got it now. If I agree to do this thing, it means you two get to see this Mr. Bennett again, right?" asked Judith.

"Well, yes. But aside from all that," said Dawn quickly, appealing to Judith's higher morals, "The kids need you. Please say you'll do it."

Judith laughed. She shook her head and said, "Well, how can I refuse? I mean, I was thinking someone should do it, I guess it might as well be me. But I didn't know that you were going to take over my calendar to advance your love life, Dawn."

Dawn and Trinity yelled out in excitement which made Judith laugh harder. Then they gave her all the details about when and where the talk would take place.

"OK, you're on. I can make that," said Judith.

"And I'll let Lisa know. She can drive with us," said Lola.

Helen spoke up, "Are you sure this Mr. Bennett won't mind if all these people show up in his classroom? And yes, I'm coming too."

"We probably just won't mention it," said Dawn, making a face. "We wouldn't want to scare him or anything. Trinity's going to do enough of that all on her own."

Bea looked from Dawn to Trinity and asked directly, "Aren't you worried that something like this Mr. Bennett situation might come between you two?"

"Nah," said Dawn quickly, but with a sly smile, "We'll be fine. It's just a little friendly competition, and that never hurt anyone. And on that note, may the best woman win."

"Oh, I will," said Trinity.

Cooper spoke up, "Well, good. I'm glad we got that all worked out. You Aunties are the best. Now if you don't mind, I'm heading up the street for a haircut. I'll be back in a little while." He turned to Judith, "And thanks, Aunt Judith." He reached out and gave her a quick hug.

Judith turned to the other sistahs, "See, I told y'all I was his favorite."

"Well," muttered Lola. "OK, but just for today!"

"Oh behave or I might make a play for him myself!"
—Judith

# CHAPTER 11

"OK, listen, while I've got y'all here," said Judith, "Let's talk about our trip to Natchez next weekend. Is everyone in?"

The sistahs all became animated with excitement. "You bet. This is going to be a hoot!" said Trinity. "Let's take my big SUV, so we can all fit in one car."

"I was hoping you'd say that," said Judith, relieved. "That makes it simple. I've got a dog sitter for Lucy, so I'm all set there. We need to leave in the morning. It's about two and half hours to Natchez, and Mrs. Melrose is expecting us for lunch right on time." Then she made a quizzical face, "She also says she has a surprise for me."

"Hmph, it's just for you?" asked Dawn, clearly disappointed.

"What are you, five?" asked Trinity, laughing.

The other sistahs joined in, and Dawn admitted ruefully, "When it comes to surprises, I guess I am."

"Also, Mrs. Melrose emailed me something she wants me to share with you. She wants us all to take a test."

"A test?" said Lola, "Oh no. Is there any math in it?"

"No. She asked that we take this quiz and send her the results. Actually, it looks like a pretty interesting test. It's called The Life Purpose Test. Apparently, you answer a series of questions, and it helps you come up with a statement that describes the purpose of your life."

Dawn looked worried, "Geez, I hope I have one."

"I don't know why she wants us to take this, but it looks like fun," said Judith as she handed out printed copies of the quiz. "You can take the quiz tonight or tomorrow and get back to me if you want to. I, for one, would like to see what it says."

Bea looked at her thoughtfully, "I wonder why she wants to know."

"I guess we'll find out. But it's yet another reason why this ought to be an interesting trip," said Judith. "Not only do we get to stay in a beautiful old home, but I believe Mrs. Melrose will prove to be quite entertaining. She's a character."

"I can't wait," said Dawn, grinning.

Bea broke in, "You know, I have to interrupt here because I can't stay too much longer. So, while we're on the subject of taking care of our Friendship Bench visitors—does anyone have anything you need to discuss today?"

"I'd rather talk about Mr. Bennett," said Dawn in a dreamy voice.

"Oh behave," said Judith, "Or I might just make a play for him myself!"

"Good, I'll take Marty," said Dawn quickly.

Judith had to do a double take at Dawn's face because the woman looked suspiciously serious about making a play for her boyfriend of over a year. "Oh no, you don't!" she said hotly.

"Let stay on track, OK?" said Bea. "Do any of you need to talk about your visitors because I would like to."

"You go first, Bea," said Dawn. "Then I need to talk too."

"OK, so I've texted y'all about my visitor, Bonnie Phillips. She's been depressed, and she dropped hints during our initial meeting about being suicidal. It's really sad, sistahs. She's lonely and in trouble. I invited her to go to church with me again tomorrow. I think she enjoyed it the first time. Plus, she's had one appointment with a therapist, and I've given her the number of the suicide prevention hotline. I don't think she's called them, though. Now, I've seen her since her therapist appointment, and I see no change in her demeanor. I'm deeply worried. I've suggested that she find a group to join or even that she take some kind of class. I can't make her go, of course, but if y'all have any ideas, I'm all ears."

"What she needs right now is something to look forward to," said Helen. "I mean, who doesn't?"

Bea went on, "She can keep coming to the bench to check in. I think it helps some, but as you know, the bench is first-come first-serve, and sometimes someone is already sitting there when she comes. It makes me feel terrible."

"You can tell her to try between nine and ten on Thursday mornings," said Dawn. "That's not a very busy time on my shift. I might be able to talk to her some."

"I will tell her that, thank you," said Bea. "But I can't guarantee she'll open up. She barely said anything to me the first time. I get the idea that she's a fairly private person."

"Well, even if we just talk about our favorite cake recipe—like mine is Chocolate Ganache Cake. Sometimes anything helps. Maybe I'll even bring her a piece."

"Who knows? It might help. OK, I'll mention that to her, Dawn, but if anyone comes up with any further ideas, let me know. I think Bonnie really needs people in her life."

Bea went on, "So, what did you want to talk about, Dawn? Is it about your Mrs. Etheridge? I hope so. She's fascinating and I've been worried about her."

"Yes, and oh my gravy, I really don't know what to do now. You won't believe what she's done."

"What now?" asked Helen.

"She's formed a gang!" said Dawn, looking around the room, daring anyone not to be shocked.

"You're joking," laughed Judith. Then noting the look on Dawn's face said, "Oh my lord! You're not joking."

"Oh dear," said Bea.

Dawn explained, "I met with her on the bench again yesterday afternoon, and my head just about exploded. I had encouraged her to join a group and make new friends. You'd think that would be a good idea, right? Apparently, she went to the local Welcome Committee group and now has a couple of new cronies. Oh, by the way, and maybe you could urge your Bonnie to join that group too, Bea. Just tell her not to go near Sissy Etheridge. At least till I get her straightened out.

"Anyway, the women she met are apparently lonely too. So, instead of bonding together to ease their loneliness, Sissy has become a terrible influence on them and is talking to them about forming a theft ring! She wants to call it the Underestimated Gang because she figures they are all such innocent-looking, older women, no one will suspect them. She wanted to start the gang off by burglarizing parked cars late at night. But then she said that the two older women can't see well enough to drive at night, so she is rethinking her strategy."

"Oh my gosh!" said Judith. "We have to stop her. They'll all end up in jail!"

"What can we do?" asked Helen, wringing her hands.

Bea jumped in, "For a start, I'll invite her to church with me and Bonnie tomorrow. You come too, Dawn, and we can talk to her together. But this is going to take some serious thinking on our parts, dears."

"I'll be there," said Dawn. Then she laughed, "By the way, that's a sneaky way to get me to go to church, Miss Bea."

"Whatever works, dear," said Bea with a glint of mischief.

Judith pointed out, "Maybe you can use church visits to stall Sissy from getting into trouble for at least a little while, Dawn. We are going to need to talk further about all this—maybe on our trip to Natchez."

"Good thinking," said Dawn, nodding.

Just then, Cooper stuck his head in the front door. "OK, Miss Helen. I'm taking off. My ride to school is here."

"Wait, come in for just a minute," said Helen, getting to her feet. "Let's see that haircut."

Cooper rolled his eyes, but walked over to the coffee bar where the women sat.

"Ooooh, isn't he gorgeous," teased Dawn.

The women laughed but couldn't help but think how fast Cooper was growing into a handsome young man. He wore his hair on the longish side, but it was cleaned up and neat. His shoulders filled out his ever-present black t-shirt.

"Are you beating the girls away with a stick yet, Coop?" asked Lola mischievously.

"That's my boy!" said Helen proudly.

"That's my nephew!" said Dawn.

"That reminds me," said Cooper, "Aunt Dawn, what am I supposed to wear to that Chef Soiree thing that Zoe invited me to? She said the three of us were going together. Am I supposed to dress up, or can I wear something like this?" He pointed to his jeans and t-shirt.

Dawn's eyes instantly met several of the other sistahs', and she saw the same question in all of them. Not missing a beat, she said, "I think if you just added a jacket with that you would look fine—kind of cool, actually."

Cooper narrowed his eyes at her, "Wait, you did know she invited me, right?"

"Of course, of course," lied Dawn. "She mentioned it, I'm sure."

"And you don't mind a third wheel? I don't want to steal time away from you and your granddaughter."

"Oh Coop," said Dawn, chuckling, "If there were two of you, I'd invite you both. Friday night will be a good time for all of us. And besides, the rest of the sistahs are going too, so don't worry about time with my granddaughter. The more the merrier."

Cooper looked relieved, "OK, then. Gotta run. See you at the soiree." He turned to Helen and grinned, "See you tonight."

Helen hurried over to him to give him a quick hug goodbye. "OK, I'm making lasagna tonight. And yes, you're welcome," she said, laughing. She reached up to move a stray lock of hair from his eyes and as she did so, her hand shook in short jerky movements. She quickly lowered her hand and hugged him again.

As she did, Judith leaned over and whispered to Bea, "Bea, did you see that?"

Bea nodded quietly and whispered back, "I did. But not here. Let's talk later."

"What the hell is up with Helen?"
—Judith

# CHAPTER 12

As soon as Cooper closed the door behind him, Dawn turned towards the other sistahs with her eyes wide, "Oh my God! Did you hear that? Zoe asked Coop to the Chef's Soiree! What's going on here? I thought they just started to barely tolerate each other?"

"Love and hate—there's a fine line between them," said Helen.

"Oh, c'mon. We all knew they'd get married someday. I just didn't think it was today," said Lola, laughing.

"Now, dears. No one is getting married today. Let's take it down a notch before we go crazy and drive both of them out of town," said Bea.

"I just never thought this would happen so soon. Are they even old enough to date?" asked Lola.

"Ha! Look who's talking!" laughed Dawn. "You had already dated the whole town by the time you were their age."

"They're eighteen, for Pete's sake, Lola," said Helen.

"Still, this is pretty exciting," said Dawn. "And I'll be right there to see what happens at that soiree."

"Me too," said Lola. "But I don't think I'll be able to control myself from teasing them."

"Do your best, dear," said Bea, rolling her eyes. "And speaking of our best, I'd better get a move on if I'm going to put my best foot forward today. I've got several hospital visits to make." Through her church, Bea volunteered to visit people who were sick or hurt in the hospital.

"We'd all better get a move on and let Judith get to work," said Dawn. The sistahs gathered their belongings and walked out together.

Bea got halfway to her car when her phone rang. Digging it out of her purse, she saw Judith's name on the screen. She answered, "Hello?"

"Bea, it's me. What the hell is up with Helen's hands?"

"Sissy, are you out of your ever-lovin' mind?"
—Dawn

# CHAPTER 13

The next morning, Dawn and Bea waited in front of the Trinity Episcopal Church for Sissy and Bonnie to meet them for morning services. Several congregants greeted them on the steps in front of the large, arched, wooden doors. A couple of minutes passed before they spotted Sissy and Bonnie, walking together towards the church. They were chatting in a very friendly manner. Bea and Dawn exchanged a concerned look.

When they got to the steps, Bea asked, "Do you two know each other?"

Bonnie answered, "Not very well, but we parked right next to each other in the lot, and we've seen each other at the Welcome Committee meeting"

"Uh oh," muttered Dawn to Bea.

Sissy said, "We don't know each other yet, but we understand each other a little bit now." Her eyes glittered with excitement, and it gave both Dawn and Bea an uneasy feeling.

The four women entered the church and listened to the pastor deliver a sermon based on lessons from the Bible but re-configured into a Saints football metaphor. This was not the first time the pastor used the New Orleans Saints to teach church lessons. They were his favorite team after all and just so easy to work into a Bible story. And to a person, his congregants were Saints fans too, so his sermons were welcome.

The pastor stood high in his pulpit and said, "I think we all know that if Jesus walked in that front door right now, he'd be psyched about the New Orleans Saints." The congregation chuckled and he went on, "In life, as in football, we function as a team. We keep our eyes on the coach when we're on the field. In our lives we keep our eyes on Christ. If you think the Saints have a good coach, just take a look at Jesus, our savior. Surrender to his guidance. Your priorities need to be in place in this life. You put your God first, your family second, and the New Orleans Saints third. It's a winning combination. We love football. Remember that God gave us football. Jesus is Lord. Amen."

After the service the women thanked the pastor on the way out, and Dawn couldn't resist a whispered "Go Saints" to him which made him say, "Amen!" with a grin.

They walked the two blocks over to St. John's Coffeehouse and ordered three coffees and a tea for Bonnie. As they settled into their seats, Bea asked Bonnie again, "So, you and Sissy have met before. Tell us about that."

"Only once at a meeting of the Welcome Committee."

"That's wonderful," said Bea. "So, you two have something in common then."

"Yes, we do," said Sissy. "And with a little luck, we'll have even more in common in the future."

Dawn and Bea exchanged looks, and Dawn pressed on, "What do you mean?"

"Oh," said Bonnie. "Sissy was telling me about a special little group of women she's getting together. I'm going to her place later so she can tell me more about it."

Dawn closed her eyes and shook her head. "Sissy, could I have a word please? Outside?"

Sissy started to protest, but then caught the look in Dawn's eyes and followed her outside resignedly. After the door closed, Dawn immediately whipped around and said, "Sissy, are you out of your ever-lovin' mind?"

Startled, Sissy said defensively, "What?"

"You know very well what!"

"Oh that. Well, OK, but in my defense the gang may need Bonnie to drive the getaway car."

"Nope. Nope. Nope. You absolutely do not!"

"I thought you were going to help me," whined Sissy. "Just when I finally start making some friends, you try and ruin everything."

"There's just one thing about your little gang I object to, Sissy."

"What's that?"

"It's illegal as hell—that's what. And you'll not only end up in jail yourself, but all your new friends will end up there too. Is that really what you want?"

Sissy shook her head, "We won't end up in jail."

"I can guarantee you will," said Dawn, firmly. "And I can't let you do it."

"But I finally have friends," Sissy groaned.

"Look, Sissy, there's other ways to make friends. I said I'll help, and I will, but you've got to give me a chance, OK? I'll admit, I'm not sure what I'm going to do yet, but if you'll just give me a little time, I'll come up with something good. I promise you that. Can you do that—give me a little time?" Dawn looked around, trying hard to come up with an idea to help the situation regarding Bonnie. She glanced through the coffeehouse windows, and her eyes lit on a stack of books on one of the tables occupied by a student in the corner. A light came into her eyes. "Alright, you're going to need to give Bonnie some sort of excuse for meeting with her later today rather than asking her to commit a felony. Here's how we'll fix it. Sissy, do you like to read?"

"Sometimes," said Sissy. "I'm in the middle of a real juicy thriller right now."

Relief and hope flooded Dawn's face. "That's awesome. OK then. You have to tell Bonnie that it's a book club that she's invited to and that, just for fun, you call your club a gang. Next, find out who in your gang likes to read and invite them too. You can call yourselves the Gangsta Book Club, if it makes you happy."

"Ooh, I like that name," enthused Sissy.

"And look, Sissy, I have to go out of town next weekend. Do you think you and your gang, I mean book club, can stay out of trouble till I get back?"

"Oh sure, sure," Sissy mumbled, looking at her feet.

Dawn pushed harder, looking the older woman straight in the eye. "Can you promise me?"

"OK, OK," said Sissy. But then she pointed her finger right in Dawn's face and said, "But when you get back, you had better have something in mind to help, or else."

Dawn's face grew dark with anger. She wasn't one to take a threat of any kind, not even from a crazy, older women, "Or else what, you little criminal!"

"Or else we're going to go through with my next idea," Sissy said smugly.

"Don't threaten me, Sissy Etheridge. And just keep out of trouble, OK?" She got her temper back under control.

"Alright. Let's go in. My coffee is getting cold. We criminals don't like cold coffee," Sissy said, adding a little grin.

"Very funny, Ma Barker."

"I could have written your answers for you!"
—Judith

# CHAPTER 14

udith sent out a group text to the sistahs that night which said, "Sistahs, if you did the Purpose of Life quiz, send me your answers. Mrs. Melrose would like us to send them in tonight, OK? Here's what the quiz told me my purpose is: To live a creative life, sharing and involving others in many forms of creativity. Doesn't that sound awesome? I love it! OK, your turn. Send them in, sistahs!"

A few minutes later her phone dinged with a text from Bea. "I just love yours, Judith. Here's mine: To live a sacred and loving life, then sharing my principles with as many people as possible."

Next came Helen, "Here's mine: Exploring and teaching proper nutrition, the power of reiki energy work, and the medicinal properties of oils and plants with my students."

Lola jumped on with, "I am loving these answers! Here's mine: Surrounding myself with and spending as much time as possible in nature and using plants to create and share their beauty for those who would appreciate it."

Judith wrote back, "It works! Isn't this a great quiz? The cool part about doing this test and sharing our answers is that I know y'all so well, I could have written your answers for you."

"Except Lola's," texted Dawn. "I would have had to add a few choice items to her list."

"Don't get started, dear. These purposes are truly special," wrote Bea. "What did you come up with over there? You, and Trinity both?"

"I didn't have time to finish, but I will later tonight. I'll just have to give it to Mrs. Melrose later."

"Same for me," said Trinity. "I didn't get to it, but I will, I promise."

"OK," said Judith. "I'll send these off tonight. See y'all in the morning!"

"Or it would have, if only Sissy wasn't such a reprobate."
—Dawn

# CHAPTER 15

"**P**ass me one those pimento sausage sandwiches of yours, please, Lola," said Dawn, reaching over the front seat of Trinity's car as they drove to Natchez. "I've never had one of these before, but I like the idea. It's got a bunch of stuff in it I like—pimento cheese, sausage, and egg on a biscuit. I mean, what's not to like?"

"Thanks for making these, dear," said Bea, opening one of the foil-wrapped sandwiches. "These and Judith's thermos of coffee hit the spot."

The sistahs were quiet for a moment as they enjoyed their warm, on-the-road breakfast sandwiches. Dawn broke the silence first, "I've been giving a lot of thought to that Purpose of Your Life quiz," she said, "I think I may have figured it out."

"Me too," said Trinity. "What did you come up with?"

"Well, I'm not artsy like Judith, or a super-caretaker like Bea, or a conjuring witch like Helen…"

Helen burst out laughing. "Witch! I love it. Wait, is it too late to change my purpose of life description. I gotta add that."

Dawn grinned at her and said, "Of course you do. And Lola should change her purpose of life to be Second Best Gumbo Cook in the World'."

"In your dreams," answered Lola, with her mouth half-full.

"Dawn, quit messing around and tell us what you came up with," Trinity demanded.

"Well, as you know, I'm an accountant, and I own a pretty successful accounting firm. Dan and I built it from scratch, and now my family and I, plus all of our employees, benefit from my business prowess. And yes, I'm definitely bragging a little bit here. So, I'll just say it—I'm good at numbers. I'm very good at growing and running a business. The Gumbeaux Sistahs Gallery is going kick ass, and I couldn't be happier to be partners with Judith in that business. It's a perfect blend of creativity and management. So, my purpose in life is to start and grow businesses, and to teach other people to do the same. As soon as Coop is out of art school, I'm going to help him be so successful, it's not even funny."

"And you've helped me with advice in my business in the past too," said Lola. "I think you may have hit the nail on the head with your purpose. And it sounds so much better than what I wanted to suggest for you—being the B.S. Queen!"

"You're hilarious, did you know that?" asked Dawn, drolly as Lola grinned at her. "Actually, I'm glad we did this exercise. It made me put a name to my purpose, and it makes me feel wonderful to know that I am actually living it. It also gives me direction for the future."

"That's exactly how I feel too," said Trinity, excited.

"So, what did you come up with, Trinity?" asked Dawn.

"Well, I don't have your talent for numbers."

"No wait, before you say it, let me guess. Your purpose in life is to bring a sense of celebration into the world, and to revere the amazing city of New Orleans and share it with everyone you meet."

Trinity's jaw dropped. "Wow! That's pretty much it, but you put it so much better than I did. I thought you were going to guess that I'm supposed to bring the finest art I could find to Royal Street and share the appreciation of it with everyone."

"Well, of course, that's true too, but you've made your gallery a vessel or a tool. You use it to meet and know everyone in town and celebrate life just as much as humanly possible."

"That makes me happy just hearing your description, Dawn," said Judith. "And you nailed it too. All anyone would have to do is walk into Trinity's house with its entire room dedicated to costumes, dressing up, and having a wonderful time, to know what makes her tick. And, Trinity, that makes others happy to be around you."

Trinity found herself choking up, "Oh man. It's so amazing when people truly appreciate you. What would I do without you, sistahs?"

"We love you too, Trinity," said Dawn.

"You know," said Bea. "I sure wish we knew why Mrs. Melrose wanted us to take the Purpose of Life Quiz in the first place. I'm glad she did, but who does that?"

"I know, right?" answered Judith. "You see what I mean about her being quite an interesting character? I can't wait to find out what she has in mind for us. I'm intrigued. Besides I need a vacation."

"Me too," said Helen. "Also, I can't wait to drink mint juleps on her big southern front porch."

"Hear, hear!" shouted Dawn.

Judith munched thoughtfully on her sandwich and then asked Bea, "How is your bench visitor, Bonnie, doing, Bea? I've been concerned about her."

"Bonnie is hanging in there. She worries me though. She's been coming to church with me. In fact, Dawn and her bench visitor, Sissy, met us there, and we all went to coffee afterwards. That went pretty well."

Dawn interrupted, "Or it would have, if only Sissy wasn't such a reprobate! You know, this mess with Sissy has really got me thinking. Is this something that is happening right under our noses? Are the prisons filling up with senior citizens turning to crime? That's where Sissy is headed if she doesn't cool it. She actually tried to recruit Bonnie into her new 'gang,' as she calls it."

"You're kidding!" said Judith, shocked.

"Now dear, I don't think it's as bad as all that," said Bea in a calm voice.

"Isn't it, Bea?" Dawn asked with exasperation. "Bonnie was all excited about getting together with her new 'friends.' They'll have a lot of time together in the pokey if we don't watch them like hawks." She took a deep breath and went on, "At any rate, I made Sissy promise not to do anything, not even breathe, while we are on this trip."

"And Bonnie is going to see her therapist again on Monday," said Bea, "And she's planning on going to mass by herself on Sunday. So, hopefully she will be OK while we're gone."

"Yeah, the problem is, what in the world do we do with them when we get back? These are serious problems."

"Try and be patient, Dawn."

"Oh, like that's my best thing," quipped Dawn.

Bea went on, "I don't know exactly what we should do either, but I think we've made a good start. I feel like this is a process, one that we are all going through together. I'm praying about it and letting it stew for a minute while trying to keep Bonnie busy. We need a little inspiration, is all."

"Well, travel brings on inspiration," said Judith. "When I get stuck, I love to hop in the car and do something different. It makes a whole new set of synapses fire in my brain, and creative ideas happen. It's wonderful for artists, but everyone can benefit."

"Yes," said Trinity. "Dawn, let's use this trip to reset our brains. It's probably a good thing I didn't invite Mr. Bennett to come along with us. But it was tempting."

"What? Wait, are you seeing him already?" Dawn asked, her eyes wide.

Trinity squirmed a bit then answered defiantly, "No, not yet. But it's just a matter of time."

Dawn snorted, "In your dreams. He's practically got my name tattooed over his heart."

"Will you two stop?" asked Helen, looking from one sister to the other in disgust. "Neither one of you is going with him yet. Please try to remember that he's Coop's teacher, for heaven's sake. This could backfire on him. In fact, knowing you two, it's practically guaranteed to."

"You're right, Helen. That's why I'm taking it slow," nodded Trinity. "If he hasn't asked me out by the day of Judith's talk in his class, then I'll have to make my move."

Dawn rolled her eyes, but Trinity went on with a giggle, "In the meantime, I have my little toy to keep me company at night."

Helen looked puzzled. "What are you talking about, Trinity? What toy keeps you company? A talking doll? Some kind of robot?"

The sistahs chuckled, and Dawn sighed deeply, "She's talking about her vibrator, Helen."

"Oh," said Helen, shaking her head. "I should have known."

"What?" asked Trinity indignantly. "Don't tell me y'all don't have vibrators. I know better."

"Maybe that falls under the heading of 'too much information,'" suggested Bea.

"Trinity doesn't care about that, Bea," said Dawn with a smirk. "She's best friends with that toy of hers. She even gave it a name—tell them, Trinity."

Judith laughed, "I hate to ask."

"I'm not ashamed," said Trinity, raising her chin. "And yes, Buzz Lightyear and I are best friends."

Lola choked on her last bit of sandwich, and Bea's eyes went wide. Then all the sistahs burst into gales of laughter until Helen got the hiccups.

"Wait, I know," said Lola, gasping for air, "Is it because he takes you to infinity and beyond?"

The sistahs fell apart laughing again then, but Trinity just looked smug and smiled knowingly.

"Don't believe a word of that nonsense!"
—Mrs. Percy

# CHAPTER 16

The Gumbeaux Sistahs pulled up in front of a large antebellum home near downtown Natchez. The women stared in awe with mouths open at the stately, white-columned, near-palace. It was surrounded by lush, southern gardens and an old live oak that extended its enormous limbs, offered shade to all. The home was three stories high with inviting porches and the mandatory white rocking chairs. The circular driveway surrounded a burbling stone fountain. Off to the side, they could see out-buildings of indeterminate purpose and a pergola bordering a small pond.

"I've done died and gone to southern heaven," whispered Dawn, her eyes taking it all in.

"Any second now, someone is going to put a mint julep in my hand. I just know it," said Lola, her eyes glued to the magnificent, well-groomed gardens she so appreciated.

"Oh, I sure hope so," said Helen as the sistahs piled out of the car and headed up the impressive front stairway. She added, looking around, "Are we in Oz?"

"I'd lay money on it," answered Trinity.

They rang the front doorbell, and it was almost immediately answered by a middle-aged women in uniform with a mischievous grin. "Good afternoon, how may I help you?" she asked in an exaggerated formal tone, a twinkle in her eye. If the women didn't know better, they might swear she was making fun of them.

"Hello, I'm Judith Lafferty, and these are my friends. I believe we're expected." Judith had to stop herself from bowing when she finished.

But the woman just chuckled, "You must be the Gumbeaux Sistahs. And you're here to see the old bat—I mean Mrs. Melrose, am I right?"

The sistahs were stunned and looked at each other. The woman went on, "I'm Mrs. Percy, her majesty's housekeeper. Come in, please. You are expected. Let me show you to the parlor."

The sistahs followed the unpredictable Mrs. Percy to an expansive room with beautifully upholstered sofas and chairs in front of a large fireplace. "Please have a seat. I have some iced tea ready for you. Would anyone care for some? Or would you prefer something stronger, perhaps?"

"Absolutely," said Dawn.

"Dawn, dear. Why don't we just wait a bit to see what's what and get the lay of the land," whispered Bea.

"Oh OK," grumbled Dawn.

"Alright then, tea it is. I'll be right back, and Mrs. Melrose will be here in a second." She lowered her voice and whispered, "She likes to make an entrance." With a roll of her eyes, she walked away chuckling, and then turned back to Dawn and said with a wink, "Don't worry. I'll take care of you later."

The sistahs gazed around at the enormous windows, beautiful molding, fireplace, historic artwork of long-gone people, and amazing chandeliers. The silk drapes brushed the floors.

"I almost can't stand it," said Trinity. "This is, of course, how I was born to live. It just shrieks money. And look at the artwork! I wish I had it all in my gallery."

"I'll hook you up with Sissy," giggled Dawn. "You can hire her and her gang for their next big heist." Bea shot her a shrinking glare.

Just then, Mrs. Melrose entered under the dramatic columned archway wearing a soft grey elegant pantsuit that matched her white, coiffed hair. In her arms was a black pug puppy with big, googly eyes. The puppy looked around calmly, but with bright friendliness.

"Ladies," said Mrs. Melrose, "Thank you for making the trip to Natchez."

Judith stepped forward. "It's good to see you again, Mrs. Melrose. And who is this?" she asked, reaching out to rub the little pug's ears.

"This is Ethel. Ethel, meet my friends."

"Oh my, she's just adorable. May I pet her? I love pugs."

"Of course." She handed the pup over to Judith.

Judith held the pup and pet her little head. "That's amazing. I can't believe her name is Ethel. You remember my little pug, Lucy, don't you?"

"You don't say," answered Mrs. Melrose, smiling. "Lucy and Ethel. What a coincidence."

Mrs. Percy served the iced tea while the sistahs introduced themselves. As she finished and was turning to leave with her pitcher, she said, "OK, now that you've all met Mrs. Melrose. I'll leave you to it then." She called over her shoulder, laughing, "Heaven help you."

"Ignore her," said Mrs. Melrose. "Gladys Percy has been my housekeeper so long that she forgets who pays her salary."

"I heard that," came a voice from the other room, followed by, "Don't let her bore you to tears with her long family history. She'll wear you out before I can serve lunch." A giggle followed.

"As I said, please disregard Mrs. Percy. Gladys and I have been together over thirty years. We're more friends now than employer and employee."

"Don't you believe a word of that nonsense," came from the other room accompanied by a snort of laughter.

The sistahs looked at one another, not knowing how to react until Mrs. Melrose burst out laughing herself. She confided, "Honestly, I don't know what I'd do without her. That woman is hilarious. But she confuses my visitors sometimes, not that we get many of those these days."

The older woman looked around the room at the sistahs and said, "So, ladies, I'll just get to the point, if you don't mind. First off,

I'm grateful for those of you who took my little Life Purpose quiz. Did you find it a helpful exercise?"

Bea spoke up, "Yes, dear. It's tricky, isn't it? I think sometimes a person might suspect what their purpose might be in their heart, but it's very affirming to put it down on paper. It was interesting."

"I agree," added Helen, sipping her tea. "Seeing it in print made me want to re-evaluate the way I spend my time to see if there was more I could do to support my purpose."

Mrs. Melrose studied her, nodding, then turned her attention to Dawn and Trinity. "Sometimes it's not immediately apparent what your purpose is. Did you two ladies decide about yours? I understand you were struggling with it."

"We did," said Dawn excitedly. She told Mrs. Melrose what she had come up with for her purpose, and Trinity followed with hers.

"Wonderful," said Mrs. Melrose approvingly. "So, my hunch was good then. A life's purpose says so much about a person, and I needed to know more about all of you before we moved on. You see, I initially figured that women who would form a group that supported each other and had the wherewithal to create such a genius idea as the Friendship Bench would be a group of women I'd like to know. The quiz just confirmed it. And also, frankly, it's that group of women that I need to go to for help."

The sistahs looked at her, their curiosity at full throttle. "Help with what?" asked Judith for the group.

Just then, Mrs. Percy stuck her head in and said, "Lunch is served, ladies."

Mrs. Melrose paused for a moment, then said, "Why don't we continue this at lunch? Afterwards, Gladys will show you to your rooms, and then you can enjoy some sightseeing in our little town."

They followed Mrs. Melrose down a wide hall into a gilt mirror-lined dining room which had been set with elegant linen, silver, and china.

"Mrs. Melrose, you're spoiling us," exclaimed Trinity. "Such a beautiful setting!"

Mrs. Percy, who was delivering some butter to the table snickered. "Don't worry, she'll exact her pound of flesh before lunch is over."

"Gladys, you're frightening our guests," laughed Mrs. Melrose.

"They're lunching with madam—they should be scared," quipped Mrs. Percy, but she winked at Judith as she left the room.

Dawn grinned at Mrs. Melrose. "You're right, she's a hoot!"

"She kind of reminds me of you, Dawn," laughed Lola.

Lunch was sumptuous. They started with a chopped green salad, then came pork chops with apple and creamy cheese grits, along with Mrs. Percy's special biscuits. Mrs. Percy filled champagne flutes at each setting with Vieux Clicquot Champagne.

"This is my favorite champagne," said the older woman, taking a sip. "I don't drink anything else really."

Mrs. Percy piped in, "Oh, she likes her champagne alright."

Mrs. Melrose raised her glass for a toast and said, "Ladies, here's to the Gumbeaux Sistahs—new and old."

The sistahs raised their glasses and clinked lightly. Helen whispered to Bea, "What does she mean, do you suppose?"

Mrs. Melrose heard her and said, smiling, "I'm glad you asked that, Helen. And while you enjoy your lunch, I'll explain what's been on my mind."

The women dug into their beautifully plated meals, and all was quiet for a minute except for some appreciative groans.

"Mrs. Percy, did you cook this?" asked Judith.

"You don't think she did, do you?" Mrs. Percy smirked and pointed in Mrs. Melrose's direction.

"I can't cook worth beans," explained Mrs. Melrose. "And why would I when Gladys is here?"

"I don't blame you. I wouldn't ever cook again." added Trinity.

Judith took another sip of champagne and asked, "Mrs. Melrose you promised to tell us what your purpose of life is."

"Yes, yes, it all comes back to that, actually." She looked pointedly at Mrs. Percy, obviously waiting for her to leave before she went on.

Mrs. Percy put her hands on her hips and said in a sassy voice, "You think I don't know all your business? Seriously?"

But Mrs. Melrose held firm, "Gladys, I know you know mine, and I know yours too. But I just want a little privacy anyway, OK?"

Mrs. Percy took the hint and left the room with a sniff. After making sure she was really gone, Mrs. Melrose went on, "Gladys probably does know everything there is to know about me, but I don't like talking about this part in front of her. Actually, I'm not used to talking about it at all."

"You can tell us anything, Mrs. Melrose," said Bea. "We talk to each other all the time about problems that come up, and it never ever goes beyond the sistahs."

"Well, good. Here's the thing." She looked down and swallowed hard, then continued, "Girls, I'm rich as Midas, but I'm lonely. I'm a widow, and I have no family. And my two best friends, well, one moved to California to be with her family, and one died not very long ago. I feel their absence deeply. And honestly, I think Gladys feels the same way. We still have each other, thank God, but I miss having friends come over. And the truth is, I'm really not sure how to make friends anymore. I know this sounds crazy, but I used to have a good standing in this community. We had parties and events here all the time, but it's fizzled out as I've gotten older. I guess, up until today, I've been too proud to admit that I'm lonely and that I need help."

Bea automatically reached out to put a hand on the other women's shoulder. Mrs. Melrose went on, "When I was down in Covington and my lawyer mentioned your Friendship Bench and your group, it struck me plain as day that it was what I needed, what I wanted in my life. I need some Gumbeaux Sistahs. And I need you to help me make it happen."

She went on, "What confirmed it in my mind was when I ran across that Life Purpose quiz. Or in my case, The Rest of Your Life Purpose Quiz. Ready to hear what the quiz showed me?"

"Of course," said Judith. "We've been very curious about it."

"OK here goes. It said that my purpose is to support and encourage groups of women and to help them create deep, forever friendships."

Dawn's eyes flew open wide and so did the other sistahs'. "Good Lord, Mrs. Melrose. That sounds like Gumbeaux Sistahs ideals if I ever heard any."

"I thought you would think that," said Mrs. Melrose. "And that is why you are here. I want to form a Gumbeaux Sistahs group right here in Natchez."

The sistahs were surprised. "Wow, that's wonderful!" said Judith and the other agreed wholeheartedly.

"Good. Then it's settled. You'll help me get a group together, right? I plan to have my first meeting Saturday after next."

Judith gulped, and the sistahs looked at each in confusion. "Wait," said Bea. "Are you saying that you want us to put a group together for you?"

"That's it, dearest," sniffed Mrs. Melrose.

Helen looked aghast. "But we don't know a single soul in Natchez."

"Well, I can get you started," answered Mrs. Melrose. "I know a couple of people to invite, but that's it these days. I can invite my hairdresser, and my pastor's wife, and of course, Mrs. Percy. We can add more people as we go along. Maybe the librarian might be interested. But you girls are going to be in town all afternoon, and I trust your instincts. I have faith in you. Go out and find our Gumbeaux Sistahs this afternoon. Start at the Natchez Coffee Co. There's always people in there."

"Oh dear," said Judith, "This is a bit unorthodox, don't you think?"

"Yes, very," agreed Mrs. Melrose. "But I think a wild card factor is necessary. Use your intuition."

Judith looked at the other sistahs and shrugged. "Well, we can try, I guess."

"I think we can do it," said Trinity. "It might even be fun."

"That settles it then," said Mrs. Melrose in triumph. "Our first meeting will be held here at ten in the morning, Saturday after next. Gladys can put together a light repast before she joins the group."

"Once I get finished serving your majesty, you mean," came a voice from the next room.

"Quit eavesdropping, and come refill our champagne glasses, Gladys."

Mrs. Percy sauntered in and topped off their glasses, saying firmly to Mrs. Melrose, "This is your last glass, hear me?"

"Killjoy," answered the old lady, with a sassy grin.

Mrs. Percy explained to the sistahs, "Any more champagne, and she'll start yelling out things like 'one more for the ditch!' That used to be funny when close friends were visiting, but since we live here alone, not so much."

The sistahs couldn't help but chuckle at the antics of these two old friends.

"OK then, Mrs. Percy will get you settled into the guest cottages now, and then you're on the loose in Natchez. Think of it as a scavenger hunt. Go out and find us some sistahs, and then I'll meet y'all on the veranda at six for cocktails and a report. Got it?"

"Yes, ma'am," said Judith with a smile, warming to the challenge.

"Betty, it's time you had that baby!"
—Sharon

# CHAPTER 17

The sistahs left Mrs. Melrose's house that afternoon and walked over a couple of blocks to Franklin Street in the historical district. They passed old, architecturally interesting buildings and shops. Behind them, they caught a glimpse of the Mississippi River bluff.

"This downtown area has all these beautiful, old, historic buildings. It reminds me of sections of New Orleans," said Trinity. "There's a vibe in this town and the neighborhood that's not unlike some areas of the French Quarter back home."

"It's really pretty here," agreed Helen. "And I hear they have an awesome hot air balloon festival in October. Also, it just feels good here too. Have you noticed that people on the street all say 'hello' when they pass? To me, that's a strong litmus test of a good place to live."

They walked down to the Natchez Coffee Co., an inviting establishment with a big, shady awning and tables outside. Flowers filled pots, and a dog water bowl was filled to welcome canine visitors.

"It always makes me happy when I see shops set out water for dogs. That's my kind of folks," said Judith. "And it reminds me. I need to bring something home for Lucy. I hate leaving her with sitters, but it has to happen once in a while. I always try to make it up to her by bringing home a new toy, or since she's a pug, something she can swallow in five seconds or less."

"And remind me that I want to bring home a little present for Bonnie to cheer her up," said Bea. "I saw a fudge shop down the street. I'll stop on the way back and pick some up."

They walked inside the cafe, and the cool air-conditioning washed over them. As soon as their eyes adjusted to the cozy surroundings, they noticed quite a few people occupying tables and loads of local art covering the walls. Colorful mobiles hung from the ceiling and stirred in the cool air. Just then a voice rang out, "Welcome, y'all!"

The sistahs looked up to see a sassy, middle-aged red head wearing a colorful apron and a big smile heading their way. "I'm Sharon Brown, the owner of this fine establishment. Are you folks wanting to dine here or take out?"

"We just need coffee," said Dawn, laughing. "We've been at a champagne lunch, and I think we're all a bit stunned."

"Hmm," laughed Sharon, "That sounds like a great afternoon to me. Y'all just help yourselves to the coffee bar at the end of the counter there and sit anywhere you'd like. Where are y'all from?"

While Helen answered her questions, Judith got an idea. She realized that, as the owner of a popular cafe in a small town, Sharon probably knew everyone in town. She whispered to Bea, "Do you think we should invite her to Mrs. Melrose's Gumbeaux Sistahs meeting?"

"Good idea, dear," she nodded and turned towards the cafe owner to ask, but Sharon was hollering back at one of her employees, "Hey DeAnna! I'm playing the lottery today. It's up to a billion dollars. If I win, I'm leaving you this cafe and going shopping!"

DeAnna, behind the counter, yelled back, "Y'all heard her! I'm holding you to that. In fact, Sharon, go buy some more tickets!"

Sharon turned back to the sistahs, laughing and Bea grabbed the opportunity. "Sharon, I know this is out of the blue, and you don't know us from Adam, and of course, I know you're probably busy with the lottery and all, but I was wondering if you'd be interested in joining a new women's group in town. It's all about making great friendships and women supporting women with some fun activities thrown in."

She told Sharon about Mrs. Melrose's idea of starting a Gumbeaux Sistahs group in Natchez and how they were spending the afternoon inviting people to join.

"I know Mrs. Melrose," said Sharon. "She doesn't come in much anymore, but she used to when her husband was alive. And of course, I know Gladys–that crazy woman! She comes in once in a while. Is she in the group?"

"Yes, she is," said Judith hopefully.

"I'll be honest. I'm married to this coffeeshop. We're open seven days a week, so I can't join. But I'd like to be invited so that if I ever do get a blessed minute, I can sneak away. So put me down, but don't expect much, I'm afraid."

"Well, that's a start," said Trinity. "We just need a few more people."

Sharon looked thoughtful and glanced over at a big table near the front door. "I've got an idea for you."

She came around from behind the counter and said, "Come with me, ladies." They followed her back towards the front door, and Sharon whispered to them as they passed two tables. "Just so you know, the table to the right is where the conservatives sit and the table to the left is for the liberals. I like to sit at that little table behind them to do my ordering and email and such. They are always squabbling over some political nonsense between the two tables. Then they want to ask my opinion about the issue at large. I always remind them that my little table is Switzerland and to keep it to themselves!" She kept moving till they reached a large table where several people were already sitting. Sharon said loudly, "This here is our community table." She pointed to a little sign in the middle of the table that confirmed that. It read "Community Table." Sharon spoke to the people sitting there, "Folks, I want you to meet the Gumbeaux Sistahs. They are in town to form a new women's group that meets at Mrs. Melrose place. It sounds like a real fun group and something to look forward to every month. They would like to tell y'all about it, OK? You gentlemen won't mind, will you?"

She turned and winked at the sistahs, "OK, Gumbeaux Sistahs, you're on! You can tell them the rest now. I gotta get back to work."

One of the women at the table said, "Why don't y'all sit with us and tell us about your group?"

The sistahs took seats, then Judith and Dawn took turns explaining about how the Gumbeaux Sistahs got started and how they came to be in Natchez. By the time they finished, the three women at the table promised to show up, and two of the men pushed hard to get an invite.

The sistahs knew the men were teasing, so Dawn, of course, teased them back, "Let us get the women's group kicked off first. Then we'll help you start a Gumbeaux Brothers group. Which one of you can cook the gumbo?"

After giving details for the meeting, the sistahs left, and Bea said, "Well, that was fast. I can't believe we pulled that off."

"That leaves us time to walk past the shops and down to the bluff by the river. I hear that's a beautiful stroll."

When they arrived back at the house at a little before six, Judith explained to Mrs. Melrose, "I can't believe it, but we may have pulled it off! We've got three women coming, and they promised to each invite someone."

"I had every faith in you," answered Mrs. Melrose, nodding and pleased. Next to her, Mrs. Percy handed out mint juleps, and the sistahs followed her to the large, breezy veranda. There were enough white, wooden rockers to accommodate them all and then some.

"I love it here," said Helen, with a deep sigh.

Lola agreed. "When I die, I'm going to open my eyes, and I'll be in this exact part of heaven."

"I find it amazing that you assume you're going to heaven," said Dawn, causing Trinity to burst out laughing.

"I love it here too," said Mrs. Melrose. "It will always be home to me, and I'm so proud of our town. We have a new mayor, and he has brought a new pride and energy with him to his office. We already had beautiful homes and views, and our hot balloon festival is very popular, but now there's a renewed interest in bringing new businesses and people to Natchez. Folks are moving here from all over. It makes you feel like jumping in and getting involved, you know what I mean?"

"I'm definitely getting a whiff of renewal in the city," said Trinity. "It's exciting."

Judith interrupted, "So, Mrs. Melrose, I think you've got enough people for your first meeting. Will you be ready? Some of them are real characters too, like the owner of the cafe. I don't think she can come to everything, but she wants to be kind of an honorary member because it's hard for her to get away from the cafe."

"Sharon, you mean?"

"She's a character alright," said Mrs. Percy. "One time I heard her yell out to one of her employees who was pregnant. She said, 'Betty, it's time you had that baby! Come on in the back room, and we'll take care of that right now!'"

"Oh my god!" laughed Dawn. "She's so feisty. I like her already."

Mrs. Percy served a light buffet dinner right there on the veranda, and Mrs. Melrose told the sistahs all about the history of Natchez and the part her family played in it. At around eight, Mrs. Melrose slowly got to her feet and said, "Well ladies, I always turn in early and get up early. I'll see you in the morning before you leave, and we'll have breakfast together."

"Oh," said Bea. "We don't want to put you out."

"No trouble at all. I'm looking forward to it," said Mrs. Melrose.

"That's because she's not the one who has to cook!" said Mrs. Percy, rolling her eyes. She then she gave them another wink, and the sistahs relaxed.

"Mrs. Percy, you'll keep us all on our toes!" said Trinity with a laugh.

"Trinity would do anything for ice cream."
—Dawn

# CHAPTER 18

The next morning, Mrs. Percy cooked up a fabulous breakfast buffet for the sistahs that included eggs, grits, sausage, and more of her homemade biscuits with last summer's strawberry preserves. The meal was accompanied by good, strong coffee with heavy cream. The sistahs were all delighted and made Mrs. Percy the heroine of the day. The little pug, Ethel, walked around their feet looking for scraps and head pats.

As they ate, they went over the plan for their upcoming Gumbeaux Sistahs meeting, and then it was time for them to get on the road. Mrs. Melrose put Ethel inside her little crate and turned to say a proper goodbye. She hugged each of the sistahs, and then she walked them to the car.

Just as Judith was getting in the passenger's seat, Mrs. Melrose said, "Wait one moment, Judith."

"Of course, what is it?" asked Judith, wondering why the older woman was acting mysteriously.

"Remember I promised you a surprise if you came to Natchez?"

"Oh that," said Judith. "I almost forgot, although I think we've actually had plenty of surprises on this trip."

"Well, I've got one more for you." Mrs. Melrose turned and called out over her shoulder. "OK, Gladys."

Mrs. Percy carefully made her way down the veranda steps holding onto the railing with one hand and the dog crate in the other.

The older woman watched Judith's face carefully as realization hit her. "Yes dear, I bought her for you. It's no coincidence that I named her Ethel. She was meant to be a partner in crime for your Lucy."

The sistahs' mouths fell open but were silent. They weren't sure how Judith would react, so they all waited to see what she would do.

Judith bent down and immediately scooped up the crate, petting Ethel through the bars with her fingers and said, "You have got to be kidding!"

The sistahs still waited. They couldn't tell if Judith was happy, shocked, or even appalled. There was total silence till Mrs. Melrose said, "No, dearest. I know you're a pug person. Gladys and I wracked our brains over something special to get you to come here. When a friend of Gladys's, who is a dog breeder, told her she had pug puppies for sale, we drove out to their country house and picked out Ethel. And it was kismet. She was the sweetest, smartest one in the bunch. Now tell the truth. Do you like her?"

Judith was speechless and stared at the little black dog who looked back at her with big, brown, googly eyes. "I...I..." Then she straightened up and said slowly, "I know it would be impolite of me to accept such an extravagant gift, Mrs. Melrose, but I have to say...I just love her!"

The sistahs exploded with a collective sigh of relief, then loud cheers. Mrs. Melrose smiled, and Mrs. Percy yelled, "I knew it!" She turned to Mrs. Melrose and said, "We did good, old girl."

Judith was beaming with happiness. "I'm gonna steal this little girl and run all the way home to show Lucy. Wait till she gets a load of this little baby!"

Mrs. Melrose said, "Now, you're going to need this crate, too, for the car. She's been sleeping in it at night, so she should be fine on the ride."

Judith reached out and pulled Mrs. Melrose and Mrs. Percy both into a big hug. "This is such an amazing surprise. In fact, all surprises should be this good. I've been wanting to get Lucy a playmate, and I'm already in love with Ethel. I know I said I needed to bring a present home for Lucy, but oh my gravy, I didn't know it would be the perfect present—a little pug sister! I can't thank you enough."

They loaded Ethel and her crate into the car and the sistahs got ready to drive away when Mrs. Melrose leaned into the side window and said, "And Helen, if you want, you can come anytime and see my doctor about your Parkinson's disease. He treats a couple of people I know in town, and I understand he's very good."

Then she waved goodbye and headed up the front steps with Mrs. Percy who whispered to her, "You just had to do that, didn't you. You couldn't just leave it alone."

"Somebody had to say something," Mrs. Melrose whispered back. "She obviously isn't talking about it. Maybe now she will."

---

Back at the car, Judith pulled out of long driveway and for the first few minutes no one spoke a single word.

Finally, Helen asked quietly, "Did y'all know?"

"You know we did," said Dawn gently.

"We were just waiting for you to bring it up," said Bea, touching her friend on the shoulder. "If you hadn't brought it up by the time the trip was over, I was going to talk to you. I just wanted to do it the right way."

"Well, hell," said Helen, shaking her head. Then suddenly and fiercely she said, "Look, I just can't stand the idea of everyone feeling sorry for me. I mean, don't you even dare!"

"No one is feeling sorry for you," said Bea firmly. "We just want to help in any way we can."

"That's right," added Lola. "So, what can we do? And what did the doctors say?"

Helen was quiet for a moment then said in a low voice, "I haven't gone yet."

After a minute of silence, Judith said, "Well, hell, yourself. Why not?" She had to fight her feelings of anger towards her friend. She knew enough about Parkinson's to know that the sooner you got a diagnosis, the better.

"Lord!" said Dawn. "Helen, it might not even be Parkinson's for all we know. Don't you want to find out?"

"I don't know," said Helen miserably. "I was just hoping the whole thing would go away. You know, all our lives, our bodies do weird things. We get a case of the hives, or run a fever, or get a backache—all sorts of things. And then they just go away."

"But this hasn't gone away, has it, dear?" asked Bea.

"No, but I'm not giving up hope that it still will. But no, you're right. It hasn't. In fact, it's getting worse."

"Ok dear, it's time to get some help then."

"You may be right, Bea."

"There's a Parkinson's specialist in Covington. I'm coming over to your place first thing in the morning, and we'll call your doctor together. OK, dear?" asked Bea gently but firmly.

Helen sighed, "OK. I guess it's time."

"And we'll give you a ride to the doctors if you need it," said Dawn.

"Then we'll all go out for ice cream after your appointment," said Trinity.

"OK, but no feeling sorry for me, alright?"

"We could never feel sorry for you, sistah. You're way too big of a bitch!" said Dawn.

Helen looked sharply at her friend, then she burst out laughing. "You women are hopeless," she said with tears of laughter in her eyes. "Hopeless, but absolutely wonderful."

Ethel let out a yip in agreement.

Bea interrupted, "Listen, sistahs. I know it's a tiny bit out of our way home, but would you mind terribly if we stopped in Baton Rouge for a little bit? There's someone I need to see, and you can all help me.

And I promise to make it worth your while. With all this talk about ice cream, I'll treat y'all to some after we run this errand."

Dawn spoke up for them all, "Oh, heck yeah! Trinity would do anything for ice cream. Oh wait—I meant me. Well, we both probably would. Let's go."

"She didn't even show up for the wedding."
—Jenny

# CHAPTER 19

"How does she know we're coming?" asked Lola, as they stood outside of an upscale white brick home on the outskirts of Baton Rouge.

"I told her," answered Bea as she reached to ring the doorbell.

Judith looked puzzled, "But how did you know that we would all agree to making this little side trip on the way home?"

Helen rolled her eyes and said, "Oh please. When was the last time you said no to Bea?"

Bea smiled innocently and poked Judith on her arm. "You'll see, dear. It's the right thing to do."

A well-dressed, plump woman in her thirties with highlighted brown hair opened the door.

"Hello, dear. Are you Jenny?"

"Yes, I am. You must be Bea…and friends?"

"Yes, sorry I didn't mention that there would be a group of us." She explained how they were returning from a trip to Natchez.

Jenny asked, "You said this was about my mother. Did she send you?"

"No, dear, she didn't. She just told me about you, and I was able to find you online."

"But she did tell you that we haven't spoken in years, right?"

"Yes, she mentioned that."

"Did she also mention that she has a granddaughter named Jilly, and she's never once seen her?"

"Yes, she told me about that too."

"And she didn't ask you to deliver any messages to me?"

"Well, no..."

The woman started to close the door saying, "Then obviously we have nothing to talk about here."

Bea reached out to stop the door from closing. "Wait, Jenny. Please just give us a few minutes. I think there are things you ought to know," Bea said with a gentle smile. "All we ask is just ten minutes of your time. You really have nothing to lose here."

Jenny hesitated and then swung the door open. "She has no effect on my life anymore. So, no, I have nothing to lose. OK, ten minutes." She opened the door all the way, and the sistahs stepped inside.

Jenny led them to the living room which was done in all white with a touch of wood and a scattering of lush, green plants. The sistahs sat on the chic, white sofa and waited for Bea to start.

"Jenny, your mom doesn't know we're here. But you see, as I mentioned on the phone, we're friends with Bonnie, and I think maybe there is something I should tell you."

"Before you say anything, let me just say this. I don't know if you know why my mother and I had a falling out, or not..."

"I know it has to do with your wedding, isn't that right?" asked Bea.

"Yes, basically. My mother put me in an impossible situation regarding my wedding, and you should hear my side of things."

"Of course. And yes, weddings can do that. People have to be very careful how they tread in giving a wedding. Feelings can get hurt, and families can really be damaged sometimes. I've heard it many times."

"Well, you're hearing it again. What it came down to is this— my husband's family is very wealthy. They are also big and loud and can be on the crude side at times. Well, my in-laws gave my husband and me an engagement party at their home. They have a big house and big family to match. The truth is that they kind of forgot their manners with my mother that night. No one offered her a beverage apparently, and hardly anyone spoke to her. They were too caught up in celebrating with each other. And my mother-in-law kept monopolizing all of my attention. You see, this family is a bit of a closed circle. They don't take to new people very well. The same thing happened when my husband's sister got married. They didn't accept her husband's family, and when he protested, they all turned on him and made the marriage miserable. They ended up in divorce after only a year. They're a tough bunch, and I knew about them going in."

"Well, my mom took offense. She complained to me and even to my husband. His family closed ranks and shut her out. My mom's reaction was to tell my husband off. Then she told me to make a choice—her or his family. She said if I chose his family, then she and I were through. She wouldn't speak to me anymore.

"Now, please understand. I love my mother, but I love my husband and child so much. We're happy together. Of course I wasn't going to leave him over this. I thought she might come around and change her mind about shutting me out. But I was wrong. She didn't even show up for the wedding. Let me tell you, that was a shocker. I couldn't believe she did that. At that point, I was furious that she'd put this stupid argument above my wedding day. Honestly, I couldn't bring myself to speak to her after that. I thought she might apologize, but she never did. Ever.

"And when I had my daughter, Jilly, did she call me? No, she did not. What kind of mother does that? She did send a present, addressed to Jilly with a note saying, 'Dear Granddaughter, No one will tell you this, but you have a living, breathing grandmother. I hope we can meet someday—maybe when you're older. Love, Grandma Bonnie.'

"So, I ask you again—who would do that? What kind of mother would act that way?"

Bea looked Jenny in the eyes with sympathy and said, "I think a mother who is sorry, lonely, deeply sad, and missing her daughter."

Jenny's eyes flew open, and she gave a little gasp. "Did she say that?"

"She did."

Jenny shook her head, "Then why doesn't she do something about it? Like apologizing, to start."

"Jenny, dear. I hope you will take this the right way. From an outsider's perspective, it seems that wrongs were done on both sides of the fence. Betrayals were committed by everyone involved."

Jenny stared at her. "But she didn't even come to my wedding. She didn't even call me when I had my daughter!" Tears formed in her eyes, and she looked away, embarrassed by the fresh barrage of pain.

"Listen," said Bea, "There's more to that story than you know. And I'm not saying that your mom is not a stubborn old woman who shouldn't have let it go as far as she did. Because she is that, dear."

Jenny looked up in surprise. Bea went on, "But it might be a good time to bury the hatchet. Everyone needs a good mother, and I believe Bonnie could be one to you again if you were willing. And your daughter might just like to get to know her grandmother."

Jenny eyes were full of pain. "I've thought about it so many times. It just seemed so impossible to make things right again. But honestly, I've missed my mom."

"She's missed you terribly, Jenny. And she's not doing well right now."

"Is she sick?"

"Not so much physically," said Bea, looking at Jenny meaningfully. "But, dear, I'm afraid she might be a danger to herself."

"What do you mean?"

"I can't really say much more than that," said Bea firmly. "Your mom deserves her privacy—up to a point. Just know that when I say it's a good time to think about a reconciliation, I mean what I say. Would you think about it? I wouldn't ask if it wasn't important."

"I'm not sure exactly what you're trying to tell me," said Jenny carefully. "But I will think about what you've said."

"OK then," said Bea, standing. "We won't take up any more of your time, Jenny, but we were passing through Baton Rouge, and it felt like the right thing to do. And here's my card. Call me anytime, dear. And if I think there's more you should know, I'll call you again." She handed Jenny a card with her contact information on it.

As Bea and the sistahs walked out the front door, Dawn, who was the last one out, whispered to Jenny, "Bea's right, Jenny. This is serious. Call your mom."

When the sistahs got back in the car, Judith said, "This was so hard. I wish we could just tell her the kind of trouble her mom is in."

"But we promised not to, and we have to respect that," said Bea. "But I'll tell you what, I'm worried about Bonnie, and I'm going to check in with her tomorrow when we get back."

"I have to go right by Bonnie's house early tomorrow morning, Bea, if you want me to, I'll drop off the fudge you bought for her in Natchez," volunteered Helen.

"Actually, that would help a lot, and then I'll check on her too a little later."

"Let's go home, sistahs. This has been quite the trip," sighed Lola.

"I even stole a nice pair for you too!"
—Sissy

# CHAPTER 20

L ate the following morning, Dawn picked up the phone when it rang. "Hello? Miss Dawn? This is Sissy Etheridge. Can you come get me?"

"Well, uh, sure, Sissy. What do you need?"

"I need a ride to my car. I left it in downtown Covington."

"Ok, where are you? At home?"

"No. No, I'm not. I'm at the police station."

Dawn, who was sitting in her kitchen enjoying a late morning coffee, jumped to feet, spilling the hot liquid. She hollered, "What did you do, Sissy?"

"Well, the gang and I..."

Dawn groaned loudly and Sissy went on, "We tried to pull a caper at the dress shop on Boston Street. The other women distracted the salesperson while I stuffed my purse with a bunch of earrings. I tried to get enough for all of us. I even stole a nice pair for you too, Miss Dawn. They have really high-quality merchandise in that store, did you know that?"

Dawn gritted her teeth dangerously hard. Sissy continued, "The other two women got scared and left, and it turns out that the saleswoman was sharper than I thought. She showed me a new line of slacks and talked me into trying some of them on. While I was in the dressing room, she called the police on me!"

Dawn's groans grew louder, then she asked, "Wait, was Bonnie with you?"

"No, she wasn't," said Sissy, then continued, "When the police came, I heard them and peaked out of the dressing room curtains to see who it was. I'm no dummy myself, so I removed the earrings from my purse and left them. When I stepped out, they asked to see what I had in my purse. Of course, there was no merchandise in there, so I gave that saleswoman a snippy look that said, 'Thought you had me, didn't you?' She wasn't very happy with me, Dawn. The police asked me if I would come down to the station, and being the upstanding citizen I am, I agreed."

At that, Dawn snorted with disgust.

"When we got to the station, they sat me down and told me that there had been a series of thefts in local stores lately. They asked me if I knew anything about it."

"Oh my gravy!" yelled Dawn, panicked. "What did you say?" She was wondering what she would have said if the police had asked her some questions about Sissy. The names of local lawyers flipped through her mind.

"Well, of course, I told them I didn't know anything. So, they gave me their card and said that I should keep them in mind if I ever did know anything. They told me when they caught the responsible party that she would probably see some jail time. Then they let me use the phone in the hall to call you. Let me tell you, I 'yes-sired' my way all the way to the phone. And, of course, I didn't squeal on my gang. Snitches get stitches and all that. Now I need a ride back to my car. I tried to call my gang members, but no one is answering their phone. They're probably at the hideout—that's what we call Alice's house."

Dawn took a deep breath and said, "Sissy, listen to me. First, yes, I'll come and get you. And second, you do not have a gang. You might have a couple of new friends, and now, from the sound of it, you might not even have that. And third, when I see you, I'm going to flat-out kill you. I'll be there in ten minutes."

She hung up the phone, grabbed her keys, and texted the sistahs, "Wait till you hear. I'll text y'all later. After I get Sissy from the police!"

"Oh good Lord," said Bea as she read Dawn's text. She sat in her brightly lit living room sipping coffee and saying silent prayers. Then she added this one, "*Oh Lord, please help Dawn and the rest of the sistahs help your poor, lonely, crazy-as-a-loon servant, Sissy Etheridge. Please help us find a way to turn her head in a different direction from the felonious one she's on now.*"

The phone interrupted her with a loud ring, and Bea saw that it was Helen. Her friend was going to run in and see Bonnie this morning and deliver the fudge that Bea had bought for her in Natchez. Bea answered, "Oh Helen, I'm glad you called. I need an update on Bonnie. I've been worried. Did everything go alright?"

There was just the slightest hesitation on the other end. "Oh Bea, everything is far from good."

Bea straightened up and listened to her friend carefully. She closed her eyes in pain for a second then jumped to her feet. "I'll be right there." She didn't even bother with putting her coffee cup in the kitchen as she grabbed her purse and keys and flew out the door.

On her way, she made one phone call, speaking firmly but quickly into the phone. "It's time, dear," she said, as she pulled her car to a stop.

In front of Bonnie's house, she grabbed her keys and ran up the front sidewalk. She didn't bother knocking but tried the doorknob. Finding it open, she hurried inside calling, "Helen!"

"In the kitchen, Bea," came the answer.

Bea quickly headed to the right and ducked into the kitchen. There she found Helen standing next to Bonnie, who was sitting at a table, hunched over a glass of water."

"Oh no, Bonnie. What happened?"

Bonnie looked up and gave Bea the saddest smile a human could produce. It spoke of giving up, of shame, and misery. Bea's heart went out immediately to the broken woman, and she reached out with both hands to comfort her.

"I'm sorry, Bea. I'm sorry to disappoint you."

"Bonnie, you couldn't disappoint me if you tried. But I know how you feel. I really do. I've been there myself, you know."

"What do you mean?"

Bea just nodded at her meaningfully.

"You? I can't imagine that you would ever try to hurt yourself."

"It can happen to anyone, Bonnie. Sometimes life just beats you up. Sometimes it can drive you to the brink of making a huge mistake. But, Bonnie, my life has taught me since that giving up is always a mistake. Life turns itself around and things get better. It just somehow does."

"It didn't feel like a mistake this morning though, Bea."

"Believe me, it was, dear."

"I wish I could believe you. I wish I could just hold on and trust that."

"You'll just have to, Bonnie, because I just won't have it any other way. I'll trust in it for you till you can get there yourself."

"I hope you're right, Bea. Meanwhile I do trust that you believe it anyway. At least one of us believes."

"That's right. I do."

"I do too," said Helen, softly.

"I just don't know how my life got to such a sad state. I always thought I'd be with my family at this point, and I'd have them to grow old with."

"We have to expect variables in our lives. We don't always get what we want, but we have to figure out ways to find joy anyway."

"Why don't you go and put some cool water on your face, Bonnie. I bet it will make you feel a little more like yourself."

Bonnie nodded and walked down the hall to her bathroom. Helen turned to Bea and whispered, "Bea, I can't tell you how close that was!"

"Tell me what happened."

"I found her in the garage. She didn't answer her door or her phone, but I could hear her car running. I tried the front door, and it was locked, but she hadn't locked the garage door. She couldn't have been in there very long because she was still conscious and fairly lucid. But she did look shocked when I opened the garage door and found the car running with her in the back seat."

"I'll bet she was shocked. Oh, thank God you came when you did, Helen!"

"You're right. That felt like one of those moments when God reaches out a hand and guides us. I think she's a little groggy and tired, but mostly I think she feels ashamed."

"She needs help, Helen." She spoke quietly to her friend as Bonnie made her way back to the kitchen.

"How do you feel, Bonnie? Do you want to go the emergency room?"

"No," she said sadly. "No need for that. I'm OK. Just really tired."

"Let's get you back to bed for a good nap, OK? And don't worry about anything. You're going to be OK, Bonnie. And Helen and I will stay right here while you sleep, and we'll be here when you wake up. We can talk more then, alright?"

Exhausted, Bonnie nodded, and Helen helped her back to her bedroom and into her bed. She turned out the lights and rejoined her friend in the kitchen. Helen asked, "What are we going to do, Bea?"

"I have a little plan," said Bea.

Two hours later, the door to Bonnie's room opened and Bea called out in the darkness, "Bonnie, are you awake?"

Bonnie turned over sleepily in her bed and looked towards the lit doorway. "Yes," she said, "I'm just lying here thinking."

"Well, there's someone here to see you, dear."

Bea moved to the side and Jenny's frame came into view. "Mom?" she whispered and moved to the side of the bed.

Bonnie gasped and tears sprung to her eyes. She reached out for her daughter, "Oh dear God," she choked out. "Jenny, thank God it's you."

As Bea and Helen quietly moved away and back into the kitchen, they heard Bonnie's smothered voice wrapped in her daughter's arms, "My darling girl."

"Miss Bea called me and told me it was time to come and find you," answered Jenny. "I'm here now, Mama."

"Yes, that's right. I was practically in the grave when my art career began."
—Judith

# CHAPTER 21

J udith drove up to the parking lot marked *Loyola Campus Visitors,* and Dawn, Trinity, Lola, and Lisa Langley all piled out and headed to the Art Department. They were met on the steps by Cooper.

"Hey, Aunties," he called out with his big, friendly grin.

"Hey yourself, Coop," said Dawn, and they took turns giving him their usual bear hugs.

Lola grabbed his arm saying, "Coop, this is Lisa Langley. She's a friend and local artist. I hope it's OK that I invited to her hear Judith talk to your class."

"I don't see why not," said Cooper, shrugging. "If it's OK for the rest of this mob to invade, what's one more? Let's go on over to the classroom, and I'll introduce you to Mr. Bennett, my teacher."

"Some of us know him already," said Dawn with a smug smile, and Trinity shot her a look.

The women followed Cooper down a long hall and into a large classroom with many tables lined up for art projects. At the front of the room, Mr. Bennett's silver hair peeked out over his desk computer, black glasses perched on his nose.

"Hey there, professor," called out Cooper, and the women moved as one to greet the teacher. Trinity pushed her way to the front. "Mr. Bennett, it's so good to see you again." She held out her hand and smiled up at him, fluttering her lashes as she did.

Not to be outdone, Dawn reached out her hand, and when he went to shake it, she literally pulled him in closer to her and away from Trinity. "Mr. Bennett, what a pleasure," she purred.

Judith shook her head and stepped forward extending her hand. "Hi, Mr. Bennett. I'm Judith Lafferty, and I'm looking forward to talking to your students today."

Somewhat bewildered by the sudden group invasion to his class, Chuck Bennett shook one hand after another. Judith introduced him to Lola and Lisa Langley.

He greeted them warmly and then said to Judith, "I'm so glad you could come talk to the class today. My students love hearing about the creative journeys and processes of working artists. There are so many different ways to make a living at art, and the more the students are exposed to them, the better. In my experience, people in the business and the general public can be so discouraging to artists, but there are actually numerous ways to make a good living at it. Even if they don't become the next Basquiat, they can still do just fine."

"You're so right," said Trinity, patting his arm.

He looked at her big inviting smile, and a twinkle formed in his eyes. Then he spoke to the group, "Well, ladies, and Cooper, the students will start arriving for class in just a second. If you'd like, you can find seats against that wall to your right." He pointed to a side wall lined with students' artwork.

Right on cue, the door opened, and students filed into class. Mr. Bennett led Judith to the front of the room and even produced a small, metal podium for her. When the bell ran, he began introducing her, "Class, we're so lucky to have Judith Lafferty with us today. She's a local artist who co-owns the Gumbeaux Sistahs Gallery in Covington. Her partner in the gallery is also here, Ms. Dawn Berard."

Dawn waved at the class and smiled at Mr. Bennett. Trinity smiled too, vying for his attention.

"Ms. Lafferty is here to talk to you today about her artistic journey. I'm sure you'll have plenty of questions for her at the end of her talk. So, Ms. Lafferty, if you will." He stepped aside, and Judith walked to the podium. Her friends clapped enthusiastically which make her laugh and wave for them to stop.

"Good afternoon. I thought today I would talk to you about how I got started in art, and I hope it makes you feel encouraged when I say I really didn't start till I was in my fifties."

There were a few murmurs of surprise from the class, and she went on. "Yes, that's right. I was practically in the grave when my art career began." The class laughed softly. "I received my Master's in Fine Arts from the University of New Orleans a million years ago. But life happened, and I wasn't able to do anything with my skills or degree until after my four children grew up. I'll be honest, I didn't even try to sell my work. Instead, I worked for many years in gallery and museum positions. But I never stopped painting, and I built up a decent body of work over the years. I truly had no idea how to make a living at it, but I always had this niggling feeling that I was meant to be living a more artistic life. It's that desire to create—that's what makes you an artist. Even if you suck at first." The class chuckled.

"But there's a little voice inside that tells you that you have to try and keep trying. It's something that says, 'You were born for this.' Do you know what I mean?"

Heads were nodding around the room.

"I was terrified about what people would think of my art. But one day, I stepped out of my tiny comfort zone and showed my work to a couple of people. And guess what? I was horrified to realize that they didn't love it. I knew it right away just looking at them, and I have to tell you, it was soul-sinking. But let me just tell you right now, it happens to everyone. True, it's so disappointing the first time, and there were times when I couldn't believe the things people dared to say to me about my work. Things like, 'you call that art?' and 'my kid could paint that,' and 'I'll give you a dollar for it.' Sometimes it was just the look on their faces that said that everything about my art was bad, and wrong, and not good enough. But something inside me just knew that I had to get past that. And thank goodness I did.

"Now if this happens to you—and it will—just take a deep breath and remember that not everyone will love your work. You have to keep working and putting it out there, and your people, the ones who just adore your work, will show up. They're out there. Trust me. How do you find them? Work your asses off, that's how. A lazy artist or an art hobbyist has just that—a hobby. Which is fine. But a successful working artist—works. So, be as prolific as you can. And try everything. Do art shows, trade shows, get in galleries, gift shops, restaurants, friend's open houses, shows with other artists, hospital shows, online art houses, dog houses—you name it. Just be everywhere you can be and learn from your mistakes. And, for heaven's sake, don't show up without a business card and a website. And use the heck out of social media, which I'm sure you're all experts at already. What an advantage you have there!

"So, I've got a handout for you. I put a lot of thought into it and came up with a list of places where artists can sell art. Go after as many as you can and discover your own too. Find out what works for you as you develop your art more and more over the years. It may take some time, but just keep at it. Also, many artists work part time to support their art, but if you can, try to work in a related field. You might work in galleries, or art associations, or museums, or art supply stores, or for art festivals, etc. If you're going to have to work somewhere, try to make it count for something other than just paying the rent. The contacts you may make could help you enormously in the future.

"Some artists choose to go the gallery route. A gallery, if it's a good one, will promote you to their database and give you an opening. But they do take a good size chunk of the money. On the other hand, they often can sell your art for more money than you could, so it works out. Other artists sell their art themselves, usually for less money, but they get to keep it all. I say, try both. And by the way, if you are going into a gallery and don't know what your pieces will sell for, ask the gallery to help you set a price. They know what it will sell for, and sometimes their price is more than what you had in mind, which is always a nice surprise.

"Don't be afraid to think out of the box. You're creatives, after all. For example, Dawn and I opened our Gumbeaux Sistahs Gallery, and we envisioned our space as not just a gallery, but also as a place for the community to gather. We sell coffee and baked goods and have a few tables and chairs. Sometimes people even hold their business meetings in the gallery. Friends meet there, and we hold social functions there too. For instance, once we had a gumbo cook-off in the gallery. It's been a very joyful experience for us. And it's paid off."

At that point Judith brought out a couple of her paintings to show the students and was rewarded, as any artist would be, by their approving comments.

"So, listen. You're young and have time. Don't be afraid and don't be timid. Have faith in your energy, your skill, your creativity, and your fierceness. And don't be so competitive with other artists to the point that you feel you can't work with them. You don't have to play the angsty, solo artist. You can help each other. Make small groups of collaborations among yourselves. You can lift each other up, and you can even do shows together. In fact, you can start doing that now—I mean today. Why wait? Just remember those collaborations are valuable and sometimes they can last a lifetime.

"So, to wrap up, I want to invite y'all to stop by the Gumbeaux Sistahs Gallery next time you are in Covington. I'll show you around and give you very strong coffee and a pretty decent scone. I'd love to see you, and I can't wait to see what your generation of artists come up with."

Judith asked if there were any questions and several hands shot up. Questions ranged from wanting know how to approach galleries for representation to whether or not art agents were worth the money, among other topics. When she finished answering all the questions, Mr. Bennett thanked Judith, and the class applauded appreciatively.

Afterwards, Mr. Bennett thanked Judith privately while several students surrounded her with more questions and thank yous. Dawn noticed that Trinity made a beeline for Mr. Bennett and watched for a couple of minutes while her sister did her usual eye-batting and giggling routine for his attention. Trinity could flirt with a grasshopper if it was male, but Dawn knew her sister well. This behavior fell into a very familiar pattern, and Dawn knew how Trinity really felt. After two failed marriages, Trinity didn't trust men, and she didn't trust herself with men. But she couldn't help but flirt. It was just how she was made. Usually, the bad men would move in quickly and then end up hurting her, while the good men, like Mr. Bennett, didn't stand a chance. Trinity was a powerful force to reckon with, and she would chase the kinder males off right away. She was either outright mean to them after a very short period of time, or she would be cold until they got tired and left. Trinity said it was because she was through with men, but Dawn knew different. She'd half-raised her sister after their mother died, and she knew Trinity better than Trinity did sometimes. She knew that Trinity simply didn't know how to let the good guys into her life. And that's why Dawn decided to do Trinity a favor. Although she knew Trinity probably wouldn't see it that way.

Gathering up her confidence, Dawn sashayed over to Trinity and Mr. Bennett, who looked to be hanging on her sister's every word.

With a big, friendly smile Dawn asked, "Mr. Bennett, uh Chuck, could I please talk to you for just a moment? Trin, you don't mind, do you?"

Trinity shot her sister a dirty, oh-we're-gonna-play-it-that-way look. She purred at Mr. Bennett, "Oh Dawn. Mr. Bennett is so busy. We should probably let him get back to work." She actually winked at him, and he smiled, obviously beguiled.

Dawn took hold of his arm anyway and walked away with the man, saying, "I know he's busy, Trin, but I won't take but a little, bitty minute."

Trinity narrowed her eyes as her sister crossed the room, Mr. Bennett in tow. She watched as Dawn seemed to be discussing something serious with the teacher. Both Dawn and Mr. Bennett glanced her way a couple of times, and Trinity couldn't imagine what the two of them could be talking about. *"Dawn is probably setting up a date with him right now,"* she thought, fuming.

Mr. Bennett suddenly gave another glance at Trinity, then leaned over and whispered something into Dawn's ear. From where Trinity stood, it looked like an intimate gesture, and she exploded inside with jealousy. When Dawn smiled and reached out to touch his arm lightly while laughing at something he had said, Trinity vowed to herself that a war had begun.

Later, when the sistahs and Lisa were walking back to the car, Trinity was fuming. She said sarcastically to Dawn, "Well, Dawn, you've had a productive day."

With a smug smile Dawn said softly, "Oh, more than you know."

"Oh my God, they're dancing together!"
—Dawn

# CHAPTER 22

**O**n Saturday morning, Lola pulled into the parking lot of the trailhead in Mandeville, LA and jumped out of her car. From nine until one every Saturday, artists, craft persons, plant sellers, organic produce growers, and food trucks set up to sell goods in a pop-up, white-tent city. People from miles around came to stroll, browse, socialize their dogs, and purchase local goods.

Lola spotted Dawn, Bea, Helen, and Judith waiting for her by the flagpole.

"Did you see her yet?" asked Lola, swinging her gaz e left and right.

"She's right there," said Dawn, pointing to one of the white tents in the corner.

"Let's go," said Lola and led the group to that spot.

"Lola, Gumbeaux Sistahs! Y'all made it!" cried Lisa Langley amid her many paintings hung on wires and sitting on easels inside her tent.

"We wouldn't miss this for anything," said Lola excitedly.

"I can't believe you did all this so fast, Lisa," said Judith, smiling. "You sure move quickly. I know I told everyone in that art class to work hard as an artist and show your work everywhere you can, but I didn't expect you to do it in two days. Bravo!"

"And you've got such a good spot here," said Bea, looking around. "Everyone will walk past this corner."

Lisa beamed, "I know—can you believe it? I completely lucked out. I called yesterday about joining this market, and the lady in charge asked me if I wanted to start today. One of her regulars couldn't make it, so she gave me her spot. Just for this morning. Next time, I'll be over at the end but still under the walkway."

"That's a good spot too," said Dawn nodding.

"When you talk to people today, you might tell them to look for you in your new spot from now on," advised Judith.

"Good idea, I will," said Lisa.

The sistahs looked around at all of Lisa's paintings, and Judith exclaimed, "Lisa, these are wonderful!" Her eyes took in each piece, and she felt more impressed with each one. They were oil paintings of restful, southern, nature images. Marsh scenes with cypress trees graced several canvases.

"I knew you'd love them," said Lola, beaming like a proud mama. "My girl Lisa has talent to spare."

"Are you thinking what I'm thinking?" Dawn asked Judith quietly.

"I'm way ahead of you, partner." Judith turned to Lisa and said, "Girl, I don't know where you've been hiding, but the Gumbeaux Sistahs Gallery would love to take in a couple of your pieces to see how we do with them. I really think we have a market for you."

Lisa's eyes opened wide. "Are you kidding?"

Dawn and Judith chuckled. "Well no, I mean we kid a lot, but not this time. You're a talent."

To their surprise, Lisa burst into tears. The sistahs were appalled and weren't quite sure what to do. Except for Bea, of course. She immediately put her hand on Lisa's shoulder to comfort her.

Lola scolded, "Dawn, what did you do?"

Lisa put her hand up to interrupt her. "No, no Dawn didn't do anything." She gulped and tried to dry her eyes. "Actually, all of you did this." Then she suddenly laughed with joy. "Lola talked to me on the Friendship Bench, and you, Judith, inspired me with your talk at the art school. And all of the Gumbeaux Sistahs encouraged me. And that's why I'm here. Actually, I can't believe I'm here! But I am, and

I'm determined to make this my first of many steps toward a career in art."

"It's a great first step, Lisa," said Judith. "Just be sure not to sell yourself too cheaply. Your work may be new to the public, but it's still very good work."

"I'll do the best I can. Thank you all so much," said Lisa, flushed with emotion.

"Come by the gallery next Tuesday and bring some pieces for us. I hope you sell today, but man, I hope you don't sell too many of these," said Dawn, looking around at the wondrous paintings. "Because I want them all in the gallery."

Lisa laughed and said, "I'll be there, alright." Then she let out an involuntary, barely-audible squeal as a passer-by stood in front of a painting looking very interested.

She whispered, "Oh my God, look. Maybe my first customer!"

"Go get 'em, girl," said Judith. "And we'll see you Tuesday. I hope you have an awesome show."

Dawn leaned over and whispered to Judith with a laugh, "These will sell so well in the gallery. What do you think? Should we stand out front and chase people away from her tent?"

Lola overheard and said in a dangerous voice, "You'll do no such thing."

"No, she won't," said Judith, chuckling and leading her friends away so Lisa could get to work. "But it's probably good we're all here to stop her."

The sistahs strolled together down the walkway between the tents and tables, stopping occasionally to "ooh" and "ahh" over the handmade jewelry and delicious-smelling baked goods. Lola bought a pot of flowers that were from the grower's backyard and not available at most nurseries. "This is a find. I've got to bring this one to Bud. You know he loves rare plants. I should get one for my dad too." Both Lola's husband, Bud, and her dad owned nursery businesses.

Dawn and Helen had to have homemade brownies, which they shared, and Bea bought a cowboy cookie.

As they munched happily on their way to the parking lot, Dawn said, "OK girls. I'll see y'all tonight at the Chef Soiree. I can't wait to spy on my granddaughter and Coop. It's their first date."

"Now, I'm not so sure that it's a date, Dawn," said Helen. "But it sure would be cool if it were!"

—✠—

"Oh my God, they're dancing together," shrieked Dawn, then clapped a hand over her own mouth.

"Good Lord, shush!" whispered Helen, her eyes wide. She glanced over at Cooper to make sure he hadn't heard.

But Cooper was in his own little world as he and Zoe swayed alongside other dancing couples to a slow, Latin beat in front of the band.

The Chef's Soiree couldn't have planned for a better night. The evening was warm, but pleasant, and hundreds of lanterns lined the street giving it a festive vibe. Dozens of tents offered delicious food cooked by local restaurants to passing attendees. Judith and Marty showed up first and scored them a table early on. Lola and Bud along with Helen, Dawn, and Bea went for glasses of wine and then plates of food. The sistahs took full advantage, and their small plates were loaded with delectable items. The sistahs were in culinary ecstasy.

"This is just delicious," said Judith, and the sistahs all agreed except Helen who was still staring at Cooper and Zoe. She said in a slow, awed voice, "I didn't even know the boy could dance. Just look at him! I swear he surprises me every day."

"C'mon, Bud, your wife wants to dance!" said Lola, pulling her husband out to the dance floor.

Bea sipped her wine while watching Cooper and Zoe and asked, "They're good, aren't they?"

TALES OF THE FRIENDSHIP BENCH

"And they look so good together—as a couple, I mean," said Dawn with a spark in her eyes.

"Calm down, girl," said Helen, patting her friend's arm. "No one is getting married here tonight."

—w—

On the dance floor, Zoe smiled as Cooper twirled her and then pulled her in close. "I'm still not marrying you," she teased.

Cooper smiled mischievously, "This is just dancing. Try to control yourself." He laughed and pulled her close. They both felt sparks fly.

"Mm," said Zoe, swaying. "Just dancing."

Cooper grinned, "Besides, after all the abuse you've given me, you're gonna have to beg me to marry you now."

Zoe choked with laughter and actually started coughing. Cooper chuckled as he patted her back gently. She finally gulped out, "Cooper Landry! You near killed me!" She added, "I'm never marrying you now!"

"Oh, we'll work out all the details later," he joked and swung her out into the dancing crowd.

—w—

The sistahs exchanged looks, grinning.

"It was quite the day," said Lola. "First our Lisa steps out and declares herself an artist. That's huge and I'm so proud of her! And now we get to witness our two favorite young people probably making the biggest mistakes of their lives." She hooted with laughter and the sistahs lifted their glasses in a toast, "To the biggest mistakes of our lives!"

"It's nice to know you've been thinking of me."
—Chuck

# CHAPTER 23

Trinity pushed her cart up the frozen foods aisle in Rouses Market in downtown New Orleans. She was trying to decide between the pint of coffee ice cream that she loved, which was eight hundred calories, and the "skinny" ice cream that was only three hundred. Some days her skinny mentality kicked in, and some days she kicked the skinny idea to the curb. She was reaching for the mega calorie jolt of full-fat ice cream when a voice came from behind her.

"Miss Trinity, is that you?" asked a male voice.

Trinity wheeled around to find herself face-to-face with Mr. Bennett, and she caught her breath in surprise. His bright blue eyes looked at her in amusement.

"Mr. Bennett!" she said, struggling to regain her poise.

"Yes, that's me. But why don't you call me Chuck?"

"Oh, is that your name?" blurted Trinity, unthinking.

He chuckled, "Well, yes. That's why I want you to call me that." He watched her and smiled.

Then she laughed lightly, blushing. "Well, that makes sense, doesn't it? I'm used to thinking about you as Mr. Bennett.

"It's nice to know you think about me."

Trinity reddened further, "Well, you should call me Trinity."

"Oh, is that your name?" he teased.

Laughing, she teased again, "No it's not, but I always liked that name."

"Ha! I deserved that," he said.

She was, in fact, delighted to see him, even if she was being goofy and feeling fat from just being in the ice cream aisle. A hope grew quickly inside her that he would talk to her for a minute, and maybe even ask her to coffee at the shop next door. But to her dismay, he pushed his cart on past hers and said, "Well, Trinity, it was good to see you. Please say hello to your beautiful sister for me."

Her mouth fell open and stared after him, embarrassed and disappointed. He turned the corner to the aisle and was gone.

She stood there fuming for a minute, wondering over his blunt rejection of her and his preference for her sister.

"*Men!*" she fumed. "*They've always been disappointing and still are.*" She made a decision and reached inside the freezer case, grabbed two eight-hundred calorie pints, and slammed the glass door loudly.

On her way home her cell phone rang, and she answered, "Hi Dawn, What's up?"

"Oh nothing. What's new?" asked Dawn.

"Well, not much since I talked to you this morning. So no, absolutely nothing is new. Nothing is new in my life, and nothing is new about men. Men stink and they always have. So, I'm done with them till the day I die!"

"Never say never, Trinity."

"Oh, I'm saying it alright. And since my divorce, I can't afford the therapy to say anything else."

"Uh oh, I'd rather eat dirt than have Bea after me!"
—Dawn

# CHAPTER 24

"Then what did Mr. Bennett say?" asked Judith.

"He didn't say a darned thing! He just walked away—again," said Trinity in disgust.

The sistahs were enjoying gumbo for lunch at Dawn's house. Bea had brought dessert, Lola brought the French bread, and Helen showed up with sweet tea. Judith brought some wine, just because. They didn't often engage in day-drinking, but occasionally, with excellent gumbo, it hit the spot.

Judith poured everyone a glass and said, "I can't believe how you keep running into this guy, Trinity."

"I know. It's weird as heck," said Trinity, shaking her head. "First it was in the grocery store, then I saw him at the cleaners on Magazine Street. Then I even saw him at my bank—all in the last two days! If I didn't know better, I'd swear he was following me, except that he hardly says two words to me—just basically 'hello,' and 'nice to see you,' and 'I love your sister.' Then off he goes. You know, when I first met him, I got the impression he was interested in me, but now he's got the hots for Dawn. Dammit."

Every head turned to look at Dawn, who casually lifted her wine glass and took a sip, not meeting anyone's eyes.

"Wait a minute, here," said Lola, jumping to her feet. "Dawn, are you dating Mr. Bennett and not telling me?"

"Well, what if I am?" asked Dawn in a dry voice.

Lola hauled off and slapped her best friend on the arm, which made Dawn burst out laughing. "Cut it out, crazy woman!" she hollered.

"Look, I don't want to talk about this yet," said Dawn. "Is that OK?"

"Oh, hell no, it's not OK," said Lola.

Trinity just looked at her sister glumly and said, "Oh well. I kind of liked him even though I can't stand men, as you know. But he did seem nice—for a change."

Bea watched the sisters and narrowed her eyes, but she didn't say anything.

"Look, you know I will tell y'all if this turns into something, but meanwhile, can we just talk about something else?"

Bea changed the subject, "How did Lisa do at the Art Market Saturday, Lola? Did you talk to her?"

"My girl sold four paintings and several prints. Isn't that fantastic?"

"Oh my gravy!" said Judith. "That's amazing for her first time out."

"Tell her to knock it off," said Dawn, laughing. "She's selling all my paintings. Thank goodness she's coming in to the gallery later. We are going to sign her up quick—if she's got anything left to sell."

"That was so lucky she came to the Friendship Bench when she did, wasn't it?" asked Lola.

"It was. And speaking of the bench, how is your lady doing, Bea? How is Bonnie?" asked Judith.

Helen shook her head, "Oh, boy. You missed it."

"Missed what?" asked Lola. Dawn leaned forward to catch the news.

"Well, you already knew that Jenny, Bonnie's daughter from Baton Rouge, showed up the morning that Bonnie made that scary attempt. Bea called and got her down here on the double. But then afterwards, we let mother and daughter visit for a long while. Then Bea went back to them and gave them both what for!"

Bea interrupted, "Well, anyone could see that they were both being stubborn. I mean, there are legitimate reasons to break up a family—abuse, criminal activity, alcoholism. But an argument over a wedding is so low on that list that it's practically underground. Families need to try to stay together, even if they don't want to or don't feel like it. And that happens to every family at some point. Everyone needs someone who has their back, and that's what families are for. Connecting to people is the most important thing we do in the world, and it starts with our own people."

"So, you gave them hell about it?" urged Dawn.

"Unleashed the kraken, did you?" giggled Lola.

"Did she ever! And it was wonderful," said Helen with a big grin.

They all nodded knowingly. At one time or another, they all had fallen under the scrutiny of their friend and paid the price for it. They didn't call her the Velvet Hammer for nothing.

Bea flashed her merry blue eyes at them and said, "Let just say that they are going to treat each other much better from now on, or Helen and I will be paying them more visits."

"Uh oh, I'd rather eat dirt than have Bea after me," said Dawn, chuckling.

"And how is Sissy Etheridge doing," Bea asked Dawn.

"Oh good God, that woman!" groaned Dawn, rolling her eyes.

"What has she done now?" asked Judith, wincing.

"She and I were having coffee over at Cafe Rani when she suddenly winks at me and slips a whole, metal napkin dispenser into her bag. Just stole it! A napkin dispenser, for Pete's sake! Of course, I made her put it back, but why would she want that?"

"I'm sure we all know by now that her stealing has nothing to do with what Sissy wants, as least not as far as physical objects are concerned," said Bea.

"You're right, Bea," said Dawn. "What she needs are friends and a purpose in life. And so does your friend, Bonnie."

But Bea didn't respond. The sistahs could see the wheels turning in their friend's head as her blue-eyed gaze turned inward for a moment.

"Uh oh, I think she's fallen into a thinking coma," joked Lola. "Let's get out of here before she comes to and makes us do something."

"No, no," said Bea slowly. "I'm just thinking about what you said, Dawn."

"Of course you are," said Dawn. "Wait, what did I say?"

"Something about needing friends and a purpose," answered Judith. "And I think I know where you're going with this, Bea."

"I think we're going to need Mrs. Melrose's help on this," said Bea firmly. "At least we need her ideas."

"Hey, speaking of Mrs. Melrose, is everyone ready for our next trip to Natchez this weekend? We've got to go run a Gumbeaux Sistahs meeting, can you believe it?" said Judith, grinning.

"Are you kidding," asked Dawn. "I am a Gumbeaux Sistahs meeting all on my own! But y'all can come too." She laughed and the others groaned, but they grinned at her.

"I can keep a secret, but Mrs. Melrose has to have gag over her mouth."
—Mrs. Percy

# CHAPTER 25

"There they are!" The sistahs could hear Sharon yelling joyfully from the front of the Natchez Coffee Company all the way down the block to their parking spot. She was standing with her hands on her hips, red hair blazing in the sun, as the sistahs emerged from the car and hiked to the middle of the block with both pugs, Ethel and Lucy, in tow.

"Y'all get over here!" called Sharon happily. "I'm so happy you brought them pups. I've got water bowls and treats ready right here for both of them." She pointed to a spot next to the front door and the dogs were happy to oblige with sloppy sips.

"Mrs. Melrose insisted that we bring them," said Judith. "I think she likes pugs as much as I do."

Bea spoke up, "It's great to see you again, Sharon. Tell me, dear, do you have any idea why Mrs. Melrose wanted us to meet her here at the coffeehouse? I thought the Gumbeaux Sistahs meeting was at her house, and that it was starting now? We're confused, and Mrs. Melrose is being very mysterious about it."

They heard a voice call out from across the street, "Don't tell them a thing, Sharon!" It was Mrs. Percy who was followed by a slow-moving but smiling Mrs. Melrose, a half-dozen other women, and one sandy-haired, bearded man in a nicely tailored suit.

As they crossed the street, Mrs. Melrose called out, "Wonderful! We're all here!"

"What's happening here, Mrs. Melrose?" asked Judith.

"First let me introduce you to a few people," said Mrs. Melrose. She turned to the small crowd gathered around her. "Folks, meet the

Gumbeaux Sistahs!" She named each of the sistahs and continued, "Now Gumbeaux Sistahs, meet your new sistahs! They're all here for our first meeting. Each of the women you found originally invited others. Isn't it fabulous?" The women introduced themselves in turn, and the sistahs recognized a few from the coffeehouse.

All the ladies were buzzing with excitement and talking to each other. They kept looking over at the sistahs and smiling expectantly.

Mrs. Melrose went on, "And this gentleman is none other than our own, Mayor Patterson."

The well-dressed, smiling man stepped forward, saying, "Welcome Gumbeaux Sistahs. We're so happy to have you in Natchez." He shook hands with each of the sistahs, and then Dawn, true to form, asked loudly, "Mr. Mayor, I'm so confused. Has Mrs. Melrose invited you to be a Gumbeaux Sistah too?"

He grinned delightedly and said, "I wouldn't mind being an honorary Gumbeaux Sistah. But actually, I'm here for a different reason." He turned to Mrs. Melrose with a smile, "Mrs. Melrose, I think you've kept your guests in the dark long enough."

"Oh, I do love to be mysterious, though," laughed Mrs. Melrose. "But you're right, Mayor Patterson." She turned to the sistahs. "We have a little surprise for you."

At that, she grabbed Mrs. Percy's arm, and together they turned and marched down the block, and plunked themselves down on a bench in front of the coffeehouse.

"Come on over and see," called Mrs. Percy.

The crowd, led by the sistahs, moved down the sidewalk and congregated in front of the two seated women. When they reached it, Mrs. Percy and Mrs. Melrose separated from each other, revealing a small brass plaque hanging on the bench behind them that read "Friendship Bench."

Bea gasped and clutched Helen's arm. Dawn and Lola shrieked in surprise and Judith suddenly found tears springing into her eyes. She said emotionally, "Oh, Mrs. Melrose, what did you do?"

"Gladys and I thought we needed a Friendship Bench right here in Natchez. So, she did the ordering, and I paid for it. And then Sharon invited us to install it in front of the coffeehouse." laughed Mrs. Melrose, delighted at the success of her surprise.

Bea and Helen stood in emotional silence. The other sistahs knew what it meant to the two of them because they had started the original Friendship Bench. They turned at the same moment and surrounded Mrs. Melrose and Mrs. Percy in a mass group hug.

"This may be the best thing I've ever seen in years," said Bea, overwhelmed, "And I've seen a lot!"

"Mrs. Melrose, Mrs. Percy, you two are true Gumbeaux Sistahs," said Helen, smiling.

"I thought so the minute I heard about y'all," said Mrs. Melrose. "And then, when I first met Judith on the bench, I knew it. I couldn't wait to share this surprise with you. Sharon was so kind to let us erect it here at her cafe, and we've already tasked some of the new sistahs to take turns with bench visitors. Mrs. Percy and I are also both looking forward to taking a turn too."

"Wait till the words gets out!" said Judith.

"That won't be too hard because that's where the mayor comes in," said Mrs. Percy. She pulled out a roll of red ribbon from her bag and proceeded to unroll it and drape it across the bench. She then produced a big red bow and stuck it onto the ribbon. Mrs. Melrose grabbed a pair of scissors from her oversized bag and handed them to the mayor, saying, "Mayor Patterson, if you would do the honors."

The mayor took the scissors and faced the crowd. "Welcome Gumbeaux Sistahs and friends. Today, we celebrate the grand opening of the Natchez Friendship Bench. We are so thankful to those of you who were behind this wonderful event—Mrs. Melrose, Mrs. Percy, Sharon Brown, and of course, the Gumbeaux Sistahs. As we cut this ribbon, may we do so in the spirit of giving, kindness, and fellowship in which it was constructed and donated. You can be proud of the town spirit to which you are contributing, and let's pray that this bench will inspire more of the same and bring many blessings to Natchez. OK, so let's do this, shall we?"

With that, the Major cut the ribbon and a local newspaper representative took photos.

"That ought to get the word out," said Mrs. Melrose, smiling.

—m—

An hour later, Judith and Lola stood on Mrs. Melrose's porch, playing their instruments—the ukulele and saxophone, respectively. The song they played was "Hey, Soul Sister" by Train. Ethel and Lucy sat contentedly at Judith's feet, accepting occasional pats on the head by all.

Mrs. Percy had served up an amazing gumbo buffet, and everyone was seated and happy to be among their new sistahs.

During the meeting, the original sistahs told their story about how they met and formed the group. They also made suggestions on how the new Friendship Bench might operate. Apparently, they would have no trouble scheduling sitters for the bench. Mrs. Percy was in charge of the schedule, and the new sistahs were eager to get started. It was easy to tell that the new group was already on their way to making life-long friendships.

Later that evening, after the meeting dispersed and the sistahs sat on Mrs Melrose's wide porch, Mrs. Percy served Mrs. Melrose's favorite champagne again, and they raised a toast to their successful day. Judith noticed how excited and happy Mrs. Melrose seemed as she chattered with everyone. Mrs. Percy caught the excitement too, and she winked at Judith as she put out hearty nibbles for everyone to enjoy. She then joined everyone with her own glass of champagne as well.

"I was so shocked to see that bench," said Judith. "You two can sure keep a secret!"

"I can keep a secret, but Mrs. Melrose has to have a gag over her mouth!" said Mrs. Percy. "Fortunately, you ladies live out of town, or you would have known it a week ago, I promise you!"

"Oh hush, Gladys" said Mrs. Melrose to her old friend. "I sure wish you knew what you were talking about sometimes." She grinned wickedly.

Then her eyes landed on Helen, and she stopped. "Well, my dear Helen, speaking of keeping secrets. Have you been to see to the doctor yet about your Parkinson's?"

Helen turned ten shades of red, and Mrs. Melrose explained, "I've known enough people who have it, Helen. That's how I know about it."

Mrs. Percy nodded sympathetically.

Bea reached over and patted her friend's arm. "Dear, if you're ready to talk, you know we have your back all the way to kingdom come. But if this not the time…"

"That's right. You don't have to," said Mrs. Percy firmly and pointing to Mrs. Melrose. "She is so pushy sometimes."

"No, maybe it's better to talk more about it here than back home. It breaks the habit of keeping it all to myself. Helen looked around at the sistahs. "I'm sorry I haven't told y'all everything. I really am. It's a difficult thing to have to admit to yourself. I guess everyone knows about it by now though. So, yes, my diagnosis has been confirmed now. And I have to tell you I'm all shook up about it. Pun intended," she smiled weakly.

"Good one, Helen," said Dawn with a gentle smile.

"You know we're here for you, dear," said Bea.

"Yes, Helen, what can we do? We want to support you," added Judith.

"Are you ready to fill us in on what you're dealing with so we can support you?" said Lola.

"So yes, I finally went to a doctor," said Helen, with a sigh.

"Well, thank God," said Lola. "What did she say?"

"I told her about my shaking hands and about the fact that it's getting harder and harder for me to walk. I mean, I can walk, of course, but it's hard for me to keep up with people. I'm slower. Also, have y'all noticed that my voice is getter softer and softer?"

"Yes, come to think of it. I can hear it now," said Bea.

"That's a symptom too. Who knew?" said Helen with a sad shrug.

"Did they test you some kind of way for it?" asked Judith.

"There is no real conclusive test for it, but I did do this one test called a DaTscan. It tracks the dopamine in my brain. A loss of dopamine is what leads to Parkinson's. The results don't tell you that you have Parkinson's, but they rule out diseases that can mimic the disease such as palsy or drug-induced Parkinson's. And my test results did rule those out. So, I more than likely have it. Mostly, they go by symptoms, and I'm a classic case when it comes to those."

"Oh boy. What else did they say, Helen?" asked Dawn.

"Well, the good news is that Parkinson's is not fatal. Oddly, one of the main reasons Parkinson's patients die is due to falls because their muscles and body don't function as they used to. Their balance gets thrown off. Also, some patients are more susceptible to pneumonia. So, anyway, that's the good news. The bad news is that there is no known cure. They don't know what causes it, and yes, it's a progressive disease."

"But there's a lot we can do fight it, right, dear?" asked Bea.

"Yes, there is, and my doctor has jumped right in with treatments. I take medication now to increase the dopamine, and I've started physical therapy two times a week. Plus, I eat smaller, healthy, frequent meals. That's supposed to help. And then there's the meditation."

"They recommend meditation?" asked Dawn.

"Yes, and as you know, I've meditated for years so that's an easy one for me to comply with. I've said it many times, you should all be meditating."

Lola piped up. "Dawn meditates."

Dawn gave her friend a quizzical look.

"Yes, she regularly sits and thinks about how fabulous she is. That counts right?"

Helen chuckled and said, "Well, that's better than nothing." Then she grinned slyly. "Parkinson's can also cause hallucinations. The other night I woke up and freaked out because it looked as if there were mosquitos all over me."

The sistahs looked horrified, and Helen went on, "But it turns out that I forgot to shut the window, and this is Louisiana. There *were* mosquitos all over me."

The girls broke out in hysterical laughter. "One thing for sure, you haven't lost your sense of humor, dear!" said Bea and gave her friend a big hug.

"And you have my permission to smack me if I ever do," said Helen with a grin.

Then, as usual, Bea brought the conversation back on track. "Do you need us to drive you to physical therapy, or to your doctors' appointments?"

"Thanks, but I can still drive for now," said Helen. "If it gets to be too much, I'll let you know."

"Well, what can we do?" asked Judith.

"You're doing it," said Helen. "Just don't smother me with sympathy or leave me out of stuff. I can't move very fast, but I can walk and sit with y'all and still give you hell when required."

"I don't think you're going to have any trouble keeping up with us, dear. It's been a long time since we've done any rock wall climbing," said Bea with a grin.

"Or snowboarding," chuckled Dawn.

"Or Iron Women competitions," laughed Lola.

"Oh shoot, did I ever tell you that it was a dream of mine to compete in the Iron Woman?" asked Helen.

The sistahs looked surprised. "It was?"

"Yes. I wanted to compete and make sure that I came in last in every event. That way I could claim the title of 'The Last Iron Woman!'"

The sistahs cracked up. "You are too much, my friend," said Bea.

Lola added, "She sure is. There should be a new title for Helen— Kick Ass Woman. She's a shoe-in!"

—◎—

The following morning Mrs. Melrose and Mrs. Percy stood on the porch and waved goodbye as the sistahs pulled out in their crowded car.

"Promise you'll come back soon!" hollered Mrs. Percy.

"Count on it," Judith yelled back. "We love Natchez and our new Gumbeaux Sistahs!"

"OK, Zoe big mouth, have it your way!"
—Cooper

# CHAPTER 26

Two days later, Helen and the sistahs sat in her big kitchen enjoying Sistah Sling cocktails.

"Oh man, these never get old, do they?" asked Dawn appreciatively.

Lola giggled. "Alcohol never gets old in this group. It doesn't sit around long enough for that." The sistahs agreed and toasted to not letting cocktails get old.

Just then, Cooper and Zoe walked in the front door together. "Bring on the gumbo, aunties!" hollered Cooper with a big grin.

"Hey, you two! What have you been up to?" asked Helen, giving them both a big hug.

"Oh, you know, the usual," said Zoe with a wink as she hugged the other sistahs. "School, work, and watching Coop eat enough food to stuff a giant panda."

"That's my boy," said Helen, giving him a big kiss on top of his head as he took a seat at the table.

Dawn spoke up loudly, "We know one thing that you two have not been doing." She looked at the sistahs and winked. "Shall we tell him?" she asked slyly.

Then all the sistahs yelled out, "You haven't been getting married!" They broke down in gales of laughter.

Cooper looked at them shocked, then turned red with embarrassment, and then he looked disgusted. "I see you've been talking to this crazy woman," he said, pointing at Zoe who grinned at him mischievously.

"Oh c'mon, it's funny," she said, shoving his arm playfully.

"Well, don't believe everything you hear," he said grumpily. His mood did not stop him from shoveling gumbo into his mouth.

"Wait," Lola teased. "Does that mean that you *are* getting married?"

The sistahs were falling over at this point, laughing and Zoe joined them with uncontrollable giggles.

"Let the boy eat," said Dawn. "And don't worry, Coop. If Zoe won't marry you, I'm sure Trinity will. She marries everybody."

Trinity didn't miss a beat, "That's right, Coop darling. We'll be so happy together."

At that, Cooper took the last spoonful of gumbo and jumped to his feet and walked to the door.

"OK, big-mouth Zoe, have it your way," he said coolly as he swung the door open. "Next time you'll have to ask me to marry you." Then he escaped his female harassers, pulling the door closed loudly behind him.

Zoe jumped to her feet and ran to the door. She opened it again and yelled, "Wait a minute! Did you ask me the first time? I don't think so!"

The sistahs didn't say a word, but there was a lot of sassy grinning going on in the silence.

"I think I'm going to have to kill a certain sibling of mine."
—Trinity

# CHAPTER 27

The following morning, Trinity sat in her favorite coffeehouse just off Magazine Street. She sipped a vanilla latte and examined her gallery's accounts on her laptop. Deep in thought about accounts payable, acquisitions, and gallery upgrades, she suddenly sensed a presence standing over her left shoulder. She turned in her chair and peered upwards into a friendly pair of brown eyes behind tortoise shell glasses.

"Well, fancy meeting you here," said the warm voice that belonged to none other than Mr. Bennett.

Trinity jumped in surprise. "You again!" she yelped and then pressed her lips closed, embarrassed over her exclamation.

Mr. Bennett chuckled. "Yes. I guess it is. How are you, Trinity?"

Remembering how friendly he was in past encounters and how he then immediately disappeared after a quick greeting, Trinity fully expected him to do the same. She braced for his rude departure and answered with a flippant, "Just fine. Good to see you." Then she went back to her computer and waited for him to leave.

But to her surprise, he pulled out the chair opposite her without waiting for an answer to his, "Do you mind if I sit here?" He sat down, smiled at her expectantly, and immediately launched into, "Trinity, there's something I've been meaning to ask you."

Trinity was staring at him in a mild shock. She couldn't imagine what he had to ask her. "Oh?" was all she managed to say.

"Yes, will you have dinner with me tomorrow night?"

Trinity almost choked. It was the very last thing she expected him to say, and it left her speechless. She finally managed to squeak out, "But what about Dawn?"

"What about Dawn?" he asked with a twinkle in his eyes. "I assume she's well, right?"

"Of course she's alright!" spluttered Trinity. "But I thought you two had a thing going."

"Oh, your sister and I are buddies alright," he explained. "But my interests in you lean in a different direction."

"Wait a minute. I'm so confused. I don't know what to say, actually. I'll have to let you know later." She shook her head and watched him as he got to his feet.

"OK, I'll call you later?" he asked easily and started towards the door.

"No, I'll call you," she said. "I think I need to talk to my sister first."

He called back to her from the exit, "That's fine, but I just talked to her."

"You did?" she called out, the puzzled look on her face grew deeper.

"Sure, how do you think I knew you were in here?" He shot her a boyish grin and then made a quick getaway before she could say another word, not that she would have any idea what that word might be.

She sat there, astonished, and then the light started to go on in her head. The more she thought of each time she "coincidentally" had run into Chuck Bennett, the more anger built up till it was nearly smoking out of her ears.

*"I think I'm going to have to kill a certain sibling of mine."* She grabbed her laptop and purse and hurried out the door, already dialing her phone. "Dawn, where are you? I'm coming over!"

"Don't compliment the jackass!"
—Trinity

# CHAPTER 28

Trinity burst into the Gumbeaux Sistahs Gallery and shouted at the top of her lungs, "Dawn! You'd better be here!"

Dawn, who was shelving some office supplies in the back room, stuck her head out, took one look at her sister's blazing eyes, and said simply, "Uh oh."

It was a good thing that no customers were present because Trinity was loud, angry, and spoiling for a showdown. "Dawn, all I can say is—how dare you try and manipulate my life!"

Dawn, out of self-preservation, kept her cool and walked slowly out into the main showroom. "Ok, first of all, I doubt seriously that it is 'all you can say,' ever. And second, I wasn't really manipulating anything. I was just helping things along."

Trinity bundled up her fists in anger, and Dawn took a wary step back. "Helping things? I don't need your help! In case you haven't noticed, I'm a grown-ass woman."

"Well, I should hope so," said Dawn, rolling her eyes.

"Then why? Just why would you do what you did? You sicced that man on me! And yes, I was attracted to him at first, but when I saw he was interested in you, I backed off. And then he just started turning up everywhere I went. And then it just got creepy."

"Well, it's your own fault," said Dawn with a harrumph.

"My fault? Are you even serious right now?

"Oh, I'm serious alright. Look, on one hand, you were telling me that Chuck Bennett was a hotty. And then in the same breath, you told me that you'd never get involved with another man again."

"And I meant it, dammit!"

"Meant which one?" asked Dawn. "See what I mean? You needed a little nudging. I just want you to be happy, Trinity."

"I'm happy enough, Dawn. And I certainly don't need a man to make me happy."

"You know, a lot of people say that, and overall, it's absolutely true. But the *right* partner can add to your happiness. It's finding a good one that's so damn hard. And *you* wouldn't know a good man if he bit you on the ankle. Coop swore that Mr. Bennett was one of the good ones, and he's single and handsome. Yes, even Coop said he was handsome. So, I couldn't resist. I'll be honest, I thought about going after him myself, but I'm just not ready. It's too soon after losing Dan."

Trinity's anger melted at the mention of Dawn's late husband. "Oh honey." She shook her head and said, "What a mess." Then she reached out to give her sister a tight hug when a thought occurred to her, "So, how did you help exactly?"

"Well, knowing how competitive you are, the first thing I did was pretend to be interested in the man. And boy, that was not hard since he *is* a hotty. But no sooner had I mentioned his name with interest, you just perked up like it was a championship tennis match."

"I did no such thing," insisted Trinity.

"Of course you did," continued Dawn, matter-of-factly.

"What else?" demanded Trinity, folding her arms.

"Well, after we all met, and I could see that he was showing some interest in you, Chuck and I had a little chat."

"About what?"

"I might have mentioned that I could help him get fixed up with my beautiful but stubborn little sister. And we made a plan."

"I don't believe this!"

"Well, believe it."

"What was the plan?"

"It was my idea to make you competitive. Jealous, even. Worked like a charm too. And it was his idea for me to let him know different places in town where you might happen to be so that he could accidentally run into you. That wasn't too hard since you and I are on the phone every day telling each other everything."

"A practice that may have to discontinue," said Trinity with a raised eyebrow. Then she thought a minute and said, "So, I get it. He shows up and acts all charming, then he inquires about you, and then leaves like some mysterious, sexy stranger."

"That's the gist of it," said Dawn, shrugging. "Look, I did it so you would slow down and give this good guy a chance—that's all."

At that moment, Coop came through the front door and held it open for Lola who was close behind. "Hey sistahs," said Lola cheerfully. "Look who I ran into in the parking lot."

"Hi aunties," said Coop with a smile. "I was just passing by and stopped in to see if Zoe was here. She's not answering her phone."

"Ooooh," sing-songed Lola. "Coop's looking for Zoe."

"Oh, please," grumbled Coop, but with a grin for Lola. "She's supposed to bring me this vintage book on botany that she has. I want to use it to get some ideas on this floral painting I'm starting."

"She'll be here soon. She's meeting me here," said Lola, helping herself to coffee and handing Cooper a cup. The two of them noticed the quiet in the room. They looked at Trinity and Dawn, sensing tension between the two.

"What's going on in here?" asked Lola, looking from one sister to the other.

"Dawn is being a jackass," said Trinity coldly.

Dawn's mouth became a grim line and did its best to hold back a retort.

Lola hooted with laughter. "You're late to the game on that, Trinity. Everyone already knows that."

Cooper choked with laughter and sat down quietly, watching the drama unfold.

"Alright, alright, you two," said Dawn, disgusted. Turning to Cooper she said, "And what are you laughing about?"

Cooper put up two hands, fending off her attack, but didn't move away from the show.

"She's has been meddling with my love life," said Trinity. She told them about how Dawn pretended interest in Chuck Bennett and then set up "accidental" meetings between them.

Lola looked admiringly at her friend, "You did all that, Dawn?"

Dawn shrugged coyly.

"Well, I can't say I'm surprised, but really—well done!"

"Thank you," said Dawn, starting to smile.

"Don't compliment the jackass," snarled Trinity.

"Wait. Just hold on," said Lola, twirling a chair around and throwing one leg over it, sitting backwards. "Trinity, I think you have this all wrong. Let me ask you something."

"Go ahead," snapped Trinity.

"OK, I've seen Mr. Bennett, and he is a looker, right?"

"Yes, that's beside the point."

"Is it?" She raised her eyebrows meaningfully and went on, "And he super nice and smart, right"

"And he's clever and funny and talented too," added Dawn.

"Yes, yes, yes," said Trinity impatiently. "But she…"

"Yes, she's a good sister, if you ask me." Then she turned to Dawn. "Don't get your hopes up. I still think you're a jackass—but for other reasons."

"But she's a meddler!" said Trinity.

"Yes, she is that," agreed Lola with a laugh. "But apparently, she's good at it. That counts for something."

"C'mon, Trinity, what have you got to lose?" asked Dawn. "I mean, what are you afraid of? That's what I want to know."

Trinity hesitated, so Lola jumped in, "Good question. What are we all afraid of? Wait, I'll start. OK, I'm afraid of dying."

"Well, no shit," laughed Dawn. "But how about you, Trinity?"

Trinity looked at her sister and tears came into her eyes. "I'm afraid of making yet another mistake. I've suffered a long line of losers in my life. Even if they were rich like the last one. They've all found some extra special way of hurting me."

"Ok, so you've kissed a lot of toads," said Lola. "Really, who hasn't? You haven't lived if you're not trying to forget something."

"I know, but who can you trust?" Trinity turned to Dawn. "That ex-husband of mine, Harry, really hurt me. And they say just get back out there, and I've actually tried to. I didn't tell you this, Dawn, but I accepted a date with this guy who came into the gallery. He seemed nice and I thought 'what have I got to lose?' He took me to the Crabby Shack one afternoon for crab cakes, and Dawn, when I went to the bathroom, he left me. He just left! And I don't even know why."

Lola gasped, but Dawn chuckled. When Trinity gave her a dirty look, Dawn said, "Sorry. I just thought of something funny. That just reminded me of our favorite movie, Casablanca, where Rick tells the heroine 'We'll always have Paris'. Except when it comes to you and your date, you can say, 'We'll always have crabs!'"

Lola burst out laughing, and then slapped her hand over her mouth. She quickly looked to see what Trinity would do and was relieved to see a grin spread over her face, followed by a loud laugh. She finally chocked out, "I'm right, Dawn. You are such a jackass!"

"I know," said Dawn with a smirk. "But I love you, Trin. And I'll always look out for you, no matter what you say."

Trinity shook her head, then smiled at her big sister. "Yeah, I love you too."

Dawn walked to the door and motioned to Trinity, "Look let's step out and sit on the bench to talk a minute, OK? We could both use some air."

Trinity followed her out, and they both took seats in the warm sunshine.

Dawn looked at her sister, "So, you're not mad anymore? You know I was just doing it all for you, even if my methods were a little questionable."

"Ha! Questionable is putting it mildly."

Dawn went on, "I mean, Chuck is such a good guy. You might actually like this one."

Trinity shook her head and said, "He is cute, I'll give you that. And I already like him…"

"That's great to hear," said a voice from behind her. Trinity swung around just in time to see Mr. Bennett walk up to the bench. He was grinning broadly at Trinity. "And just so you know, the feeling is mutual."

Trinity turned beet red and turned on her sister, "Dawn, you did it again?"

"Yes. I told him you were coming over here, gunning for me. He insisted on coming over to explain things to you."

Trinity looked back at him, amazed, as he said, "Dawn's right, and I'm sorry. We won't do it again if you'll agree to go across the street and have a cup of coffee with me so I can tell you everything."

Trinity looked at him and made a decision. She gathered herself up royally and the old Trinity came into her eyes. "Oh yes, you will. And from the beginning too." She strutted past him, and he followed grinning as he gave Dawn a big thumbs-up.

Just then, Cooper, who had been watching from the window, stuck his head out of the front door and yelled, "Hey Mr. Bennett! Just so you know—she'll say she won't marry you, but don't believe a word of it. That's just what these women do." Cooper doubled over with laughter as Lola and Dawn looked at him, horrified.

Then he added, "Yeah, maybe now you'll leave Zoe and me alone."

"Oh please," said Dawn, grinning. "That just means you'll have to get married now."

Cooper threw his hands up in disgust.

"She'll probably have them stealing cars
in the parking lot before long."
—Dawn

# CHAPTER 29

At the end of the week, the sistahs met at the gallery with Bonnie, Sissy, and Linda. Judith served coffee and Helen passed around homemade scones. Sissy took three and put two in her purse while Helen laughed. Dawn scowled at her while Sissy said, "Oh c'mon. At least this is legal."

Then Bea began. "So, we have an idea to share with you," she said to Bonnie, Sissy, and Linda.

"You're gonna love it," assured Lola.

"The thing is, it's been our experience that there are few things in life that bring joy and laughter than having a good group of women friends."

"Hear, hear!" yelled Dawn.

"And forming a new Gumbeaux Sistahs group in Natchez gave us an idea. We want to help you three form your own new Gumbeaux Sistahs group too."

"That would be wonderful," said Linda enthusiastically, and Bonnie smiled in agreement.

Sissy, looking panicked and said, "I don't know if I'm ready for that."

Bea looked at her in surprise and Dawn stepped in, "What do you mean, Sissy? You would love this. Why would you object to it?"

Sissy looked uncomfortable, then embarrassed. Then she blurted out, "Are you kidding? I'm practically a criminal! Who would want to hang out with me? After all I've done? These women are nice folks, and y'all know that I'm a bad influence, apparently." Sissy looked as if she was on the verge of tears.

Bea watched her carefully and felt her heart melt. She glanced at Dawn and then said, "Sissy, let me tell you a story. I read a fascinating article recently about a South African tradition they call Ubuntu. It works like this: when someone in a village does something wrong or even commits a crime, the whole village surrounds that person, and everyone has to say something nice about them. In that way, the person can regain a sense of their goodness and worth. It's a beautiful ceremony, and I'm thinking that it's what we need to do right now here for you."

"Good idea, Bea," said Judith.

The sistahs nodded in agreement, but Sissy said, "Oh God! No one will be able to think of a single thing nice about me. I'm not sure I could myself."

"You just watch," said Dawn. "I'll start." She faced her with a smile. "Sissy, if I know one thing about you, it's that you are creative. I haven't met one other person on the Friendship Bench who had problems and decided to solve them with crime."

Sissy chuckled along with Dawn, and then Bea said, "Here's what I think, Sissy. I think you talk about all this crime and bad deeds, but I can sense a good heart a mile away."

At that, Sissy smiled, and her eyes shone. Lola went next. "I love hearing Dawn's stories about you, Sissy. They made my day a couple of times. I can just imagine what kind of ideas you'll come up with if you took that imagination of yours in a different direction."

Sissy raised her eyebrows and mused on that thoughtfully.

It was Judith's turn, so she said, "Sissy, you brought a lot of life to our group. You have a lot of great energy to share."

And Helen jumped in, "And anyone who likes scones as much as you do can't be half bad, Sissy." She pointed to the purse where Sissy had hidden two scones. Sissy blushed, but then grinned.

Finally, Bonnie and Linda spoke up. Bonnie started with, "Sissy, hanging around you has perked up my own life. I always look forward to seeing you."

Linda added, "That's right, Sissy. I feel the same way. If we form this Gumbeaux Sistahs group, it just wouldn't be the same without you."

And then the tears did come. Sissy looked around the room with a wavering voice and said, "You people. If you keep this up, you're gonna ruin my gangsta reputation." She smiled through her tears.

Two weeks later the sistahs filled the cafe area of the Gumbeaux Sistahs Gallery. In addition, Bonnie, Sissy, and Linda were there with five other women from the Welcome Committee who were there by invitation. Even Zoe was present. It was a mixed bag of women and a joyful one. The women were happy to have been invited not only for the company, but also because Bea was serving her mom's gumbo.

After bowls of the hot concoction were handed around, Dawn stood before the group and welcomed them. "Ladies, we are so glad you could make it. We welcome you to the first meeting of Gumbeaux Sistahs Group number three!"

"Yeah, baby!" hollered Lola, and Bea shushed her, laughing.

"If you're in the mood for fun, good food, company, adventures, and deep, long-lasting friendship, you're in the right place. And if you're not, well, I promise you will be soon enough."

The women chuckled. Dawn could tell that Sissy was excited by the new sparkle in her eyes as she introduced her, "I'm going to turn this meeting over to Sissy Etheridge now, who has volunteered to—"

"You mean I had my arm twisted!" Sissy interrupted.

"Same thing," laughed Dawn. "Anyway, she's volunteered to be your Coordinator for the first year, and then after that, you need to vote someone else into the position. Taking turns at this is what it's all about. It keeps things fresh and, well, just interesting."

Sissy came to the front of the room and looked around. With all the attention she suddenly got a deer-in-the-headlights look, and so Dawn prompted her, "Sissy's going to tell y'all how the group works."

Sissy swallowed and spoke softly at first. "The Gumbeaux Sistahs is all about sisterhood. We will want to support each other personally as well as in business. Plus, we want to have a great time and make wonderful memories." As she spoke, Sissy grew more confident. "We will meet for coffee or cocktails or a meal on the first Thursday of each month. We can meet at restaurants or other places or if someone wants to invite us over to their house, we can do that too. Then, every other month, we'll have an activity—or as I like to call them, an adventure. Now, since I'm your coordinator, I've made a list of activities we can do, but please, I want your suggestions at all times. So far, I've come up with the following. We can attend a cooking class together. Then we can go kayaking another time. And I think a swamp boat tour might be in order. Does that sound like fun? I encourage everyone to take part in the adventures and especially in the meetings. You won't want to miss out."

She went on, "Also, we have to decide how big our group should get. The advantage of a large group is, of course, the more the merrier. The advantage of a small group is that it's easier to make reservations for activities and restaurants and to find a place to meet. And before we go any further, I want to take our first sistahs' picture. That's where Trinity comes in."

Trinity hurried to the front of the room with a big box in her hands. "For our first picture, I've brought something for everyone to borrow, but I think the group should get their own props eventually. That way, whenever you take pictures, you can get them out and make it a party." She reached into the box and pulled out bright, multi-colored feather boas and hats.

"Ooh," said Judith. "Looks like a party to me!"

Trinity handed out the colorful items to each woman, and then she stood back and watched as they transformed each woman into a diva.

"OK sistahs, let's scoot over this way, and everyone give me a big smile. Zoe, who was also wearing a boa, took the shot. Afterwards she told Dawn, "I could get used to wearing this. You know, I was thinking about getting a few of my friends together who are my age for our own Gumbeaux Sistahs group.

"Good idea," said Dawn.

"But I don't know how to cook gumbo," she said, giving her grandmother a side eye hint.

Dawn looked at her and laughed. "Nice try. But I will teach you how to make your own. It's time you learned."

The original sistahs stood to one side happily watching new friendships form. Lola leaned over to Dawn and whispered, "It was a great idea making Sissy the Coordinator. That should keep her out of trouble!"

Dawn answered, "Either that, or we just formed the Gumbeaux Sistahs Gang. She might have them all stealing cars in the parking lot before long."

Lola slapped her hand to her forehead. "Oh my gravy, surely not!"

Helen joined in, with a smile, "You know if we keep starting these groups, pretty soon you won't be able to throw a rock without hitting a Gumbeaux Sistah."

Lola chuckled and said, "Make sure you throw it in Dawn's direction. I'll help you."

"I wonder who will show up next."
—Bea

# CHAPTER 30

After the meeting, all the original Gumbeaux Sistahs hung around to clean up. Judith pulled out a bottle of wine from the mini fridge to help with the winding down.

As Trinity collected trash off the tables with a black garbage bag, she said, "Well sistahs, I think that went pretty darned well."

"I know. I kind of wanted to join this new group too, didn't you?" Lola said, laughing. "It sounds like they are going to have so much fun together, and they had some great adventure ideas. Then I remembered y'all. You're pretty much fun too."

"They are a great group of women," agreed Helen, moving slowly, but still helping her friends. "I can't wait to watch them grow their friendships."

Suddenly, Trinity got a secret little smile across her face and Dawn noticed, of course. "What's up with you, Trinity? You look like a canary-stuffed cat. What's going on?"

Trinity looked at her coyly. "Oh well, I was just thinking about last night."

"Ooh, that's right," said Dawn. "You were out with Chuck again last night, weren't you?"

Trinity blushed slightly and her eyes shone. "Yep, I sure was."

Dawn stared at her sister, reading her expression. "You really like him, don't you? I haven't seen you look like that since that time I made you a chocolate ganache cake."

"Oh, leave her alone, Dawn," said Lola, grinning. "I mean, just because the woman looks like she might burst into song at any moment." And at that, Lola did just that. She stood and belted out a loud, slightly off-key *"I'm in love, I'm in love, I'm in love with a wonderful guy!"*

At that, all of the sistahs joined in singing loudly, and then surprisingly, so did Trinity. She broke it off, laughing. "OK, people. Just knock it off. Yes, Chuck and I are having a blast, but I don't want you meddlers jinxing it. I mean, there's been enough meddling as it is." She looked pointedly at Dawn.

"OK, OK," said Dawn, but added, "You can thank me for all my meddling at the wedding." The sistahs burst out laughing until Bea calmed them all down.

She said, "C'mon girls, leave Trinity alone." But then, to everyone's surprise, she added, "But I for one cannot wait to dance at your wedding, Trinity."

Trinity's eyes bugged out. "Not you too, Bea!"

"Sorry, couldn't resist," said Bea, smiling gently. "Just know that we're happy you're happy."

Judith was standing at the front door looking out the window and said, "You know, it's a gorgeous evening. Why don't we sit out front and enjoy it together for a little while."

The sistahs agreed it was a great idea, and they filed outside. They scrunched as many of them as they could fit on the Friendship Bench, laughing. Dawn and Trinity stood behind the rest as they scooted in together and relaxed, breathing in the cool air. The last of the sun's rays glowed on their upturned faces. Sighing, they looked around to see people heading home from work and strolling through shops. A couple of cars drove by, and one or two drivers waved at the sistahs.

"I love this place," sighed Helen.

"Me too," said Judith. "I can't believe how lucky we are to be here, and how lucky we are to have each other. And I still can't believe that y'all chose me to be one of your sistahs. It's one of the best things to ever happen to me."

"Oh, don't you get all mushy on me, Judith, or you'll have us all crying," said Dawn. "It's way too nice a day for that. And besides, you'll scare away any new Friendship Bench visitors who may show up."

At that, the sistahs all looked carefully up and down their crepe myrtle-lined street. Bea added with a contented sigh, "I wonder who will show up next."

*The End*

# GUMBEAUX SISTAHS' RECIPES

# Mrs. Percy's Pork Chops with Apples and Creamy Cheese Grits

6 whole Boneless Pork Chops, about 1/2-inch Thick
2 tablespoons Olive Oil
2 tablespoons Butter
2 whole Gala Apples, Diced
1/2 cup Dry White Wine
2 teaspoons Apple Cider Vinegar
3/4 cups Pure Maple Syrup
1 dash Salt
Freshly Ground Black Pepper

## INSTRUCTIONS

1.  Heat a large, heavy skillet over medium-high heat. Add olive oil and butter and heat until butter is melted.
2.  Salt and pepper both sides of pork chops. Brown them on both sides until nice and golden. Remove pork chops from the skillet and set on a separate plate.
3.  Reduce heat to medium. Add apples and stir to combine them with the oil and butter that remain in the pan. Pour in wine and vinegar, then whisk along the bottom of the pan to deglaze it. Cook until liquid is reduced by half, about 5 minutes. Pour in the maple syrup, then add a dash of salt and pepper. Stir, then return pork chops to the pan. Cover the pan and simmer on low for 20 minutes
4.  Serve pork chops on top of a generous helping of Creamy Cheese Grits and spoon the apple-maple sauce over the top, allowing the liquid to drip over the grits.

## Creamy Cheese Grits

*   2 teaspoons coarse kosher salt
*   1 cup fine quick-cooking grits (not instant)

- 1 1/4 cups half and half
- 2 tablespoons unsalted butter
- 1 1/2 cups sharp cheddar cheese, grated
- 1/2 teaspoon freshly ground black pepper
- 1/2 cup scallions, chopped, for garnish
- sharp cheddar cheese for garnish

## Instructions

- Bring 4 cups of water to a boil in a large, heavy-bottom saucepan.
- Add the Kosher salt and then slowly add the quick cooking grits, stirring constantly. Reduce the heat to low and simmer, stirring occasionally, until the grits thicken, approximately 5 to 7 minutes.
- Stir in the half-and-half and butter to the grits. The mixture will thicken as it cooks. Bring back up to a low simmer.
- Cover the pot and reduce the heat to low for 30-45 minutes, stirring occasionally.
- Take the saucepan off the heat and fold in the cheddar cheese.
- Garnish with additional grated cheddar cheese and scallions.
- Serves 6

# Classic New Orleans Style Bread Pudding with Bourbon Sauce

**Yield:** 10 to 12 servings

12 to 14 cups of 1-inch cubes of day-old white bread, such as French or Italian. (Some people like to add day old cake into the mix to replace some of the bread. Bread Pudding can be a creative endeavor!)

7 tablespoons butter

2 cups heavy cream

4 cups whole milk

6 large eggs

1 3/4 cups plus 2 tablespoons light brown sugar

4 1/2 teaspoons vanilla extract

1 1/2 teaspoons ground cinnamon

1/2 teaspoon freshly grated nutmeg

1/4 teaspoon salt

1/2 cup raisins (if desired)

Confectioners' sugar, for garnish

Whiskey Sauce (see below)

## Directions

- Preheat the oven to 350F.
- Place the bread in a large bowl. In a small saucepan, melt 6 tablespoons butter and pour over the bread cubes. Use a rubber spatula to toss the bread and evenly distribute the butter. Grease a 9 x 13-inch casserole dish with the remaining tablespoon of butter and set aside.
- Combine the heavy cream, milk, eggs, brown sugar, vanilla, cinnamon, nutmeg, salt, and raisins in a large bowl. Whisk to mix. Pour the cream mixture over the bread and stir to combine. Allow the mixture to sit at room temperature for 30 to 45 minutes.

- Transfer the bread mixture to the casserole dish and bake until the center of the bread pudding is set, 50 to 60 minutes.
- Garnish the bread pudding with confectioners' sugar and serve warm with warm Whiskey Sauce.

## Whiskey Sauce

- 2 cups heavy cream
- 1/2 cup whole milk
- 1/2 cup granulated sugar
- 2 tablespoons cornstarch
- 3/4 cup bourbon or other whiskey
- Pinch of salt
- 2 tablespoons butter

## Directions

- In a 1-quart saucepan at medium heat, combine the cream, milk, and sugar. Place the cornstarch and 1/4 cup of the bourbon in a small mixing bowl and whisk to blend. Pour the mixture into the cream mixture and bring to a boil. Once the sauce begins to boil, reduce the heat to a gentle simmer and cook, stirring occasionally, for 5 minutes. Remove the sauce from the heat, add the salt, and stir in the butter and the remaining 1/2 cup of bourbon. Serve warm. Note: A little taste of bourbon while you're cooking doesn't hurt either!

# Judith's Quick Pimento Cheese, Sausage, and Fried Egg Breakfast Sandwich

## Ingredients:

1 cup mayonnaise
2 small cloves of garlic, minced
½ teaspoon cayenne pepper
3 cups (12 oz) shredded sharp cheddar cheese
½ cup pimientos, diced, well-drained from jar
1 pound (1 roll) of pork sausage
1 package (1 roll) of large, refrigerated buttermilk biscuits
10 eggs


For pimiento cheese spread, combine mayonnaise, garlic and cayenne pepper; mix well. Stir in cheese and pimientos; mix well. Refrigerate at least 30 minute or up to 3 days.

Cook biscuits according to directions on package.

Make sausage into 10 patties and cook in pan till brown and no pink is showing on inside.

Fry 10 eggs.

To serve: Spread 1 1/2 tablespoons of pimiento cheese spread over each half of biscuit. Place sausage patty on bottom of biscuit, top with fried egg and biscuit top. Wonderful for brunch, and they travel well wrapped in foil and placed in cooler.

# Dawn's Easy Dark Chocolate Ganache Tart

Super easy. The filling is made in the microwave and the crust is crushed up cookies!

**Servings** 12

## Ingredients

### For the Crust

2 cups cookie crumbs—short bread, chocolate or any kind of cookie, shortbread, or graham cracker will work
7 tablespoons butter
3 tablespoons granulated sugar

### For Chocolate Ganache Filling

14 ounces dark chocolate, cut into chunks, plus an extra handful for garnish
10 ounces heavy whipping cream
5 tablespoons butter, cubed
1/4 teaspoon kosher salt
coarse salt for garnish
salted caramel sauce for garnish (I use store-bought in a jar for this easy dessert version)

## Instructions

1. Preheat oven to 350 degrees. Spray 11' tart pan with nonstick spray.
2. Crush cookies into a fine consistency. I used a food processor, but you can also put them in a Ziploc type bag and crush with a rolling pin
3. Combine crumbs with 7 tablespoons melted butter and 1/3 cup sugar. Press into tart pan

4.  Bake for 8-10 minutes. Completely cool
5.  Put chocolate chunks in large mixing bowl and top with 5 tablespoons cubed butter and 1/4 teaspoon kosher salt
6.  Heat the 10 ounces of heavy cream in microwave safe container for 2 minutes. (I just use my measuring cup)
7.  Pour over the chocolate and butter. Do not stir. Cover with plastic wrap and let sit for 5 minutes
8.  Using a wire whisk, mix until smooth
9.  Pour into cooled cookie crust and spread evenly with spatula
10. Cool for two hours in refrigerator or overnight
11. Brush top with 1 teaspoon vegetable oil for a shiny appearance if desired. Top with additional chopped chocolate, coarse salt and caramel sauce if desired.

Don't forget to recommend
**_Tales of the Friendship Bench_**
for your next book club meeting!

Reading group guide available at
www.gumbeauxsistahs.com

# FINDING THE PURPOSE OF YOUR LIFE QUIZ

### By Jax Frey

**H**ow does it feel to be living according to your life's purpose? As you have already sensed, there is a very good reason to pursue that answer. Knowing your life's purpose will enlighten your life and bring you to higher levels of clarity, serenity, and especially happiness. Knowing and living your life purpose will bring you to enthusiasm, true excitement, and joy. There is a sense of belonging and of being in the right place in the universe. Unhappiness—and its ugly relations of physical, spiritual, and emotional illness—begins to dissolve from your life. Therefore, it should be your main concern. Your true focus.

## Clues

Right off the bat, do not expect your current job or career to be the final answer to the question of your life's purpose. Many people make the mistake of thinking that their work is their life. That's a trap. However, you can often incorporate your purpose into your current job. Another thing to keep in mind is that our true purposes can often be muddled with our self-esteem, and we allow the opinions of others to dictate what we are, who we become, and what we do. This can be extremely limiting.

In addition, we often think in terms, especially when we are young, that we have a grand destiny, a revolutionary path. However, your destiny may lie in simply being true to a value that you hold the most dear. Obviously, one of the first steps in knowing our life's purpose is to know WHO WE ARE—the person for whom the destiny lies waiting.

Some of you have a fairly good grasp on many aspects about Who You Are and will therefore be able to move forward with finding the purpose of your life.

For some of you, that answer may not be so simple. If your purpose does not crystallize itself right away, the following are some suggestions to help you to continue on a quest to find out who you are. Be encouraged, however, because taking this test will be an exercise in clarity itself.

## Suggestions for taking this test:

- List those things that you are really good at and what makes you feel wonderful.
- Look within through meditation, prayer, journaling, or any other activity that brings you inner peace.
- Do what makes you happy and see where it takes you. Let your intuition guide you.
- Examine the clues of your life such as patterns, decisions, choices, and passions.

- Heal yourself. Remove the old patterns and blockages. Face your angers and become whole.
- Revisit the dreams and desires of your childhood.
- Look at where you are spending your free time.
- Do creativity exercises.

## First Steps

Accepting that you do have a special purpose in life is the first step. You must create an intention to find your purpose and act on it—and be committed to doing so. Commit to finding out what you are supposed to be doing and be open to what you may find. Don't be surprised if you are already doing a form of it because it is part of who you are. And if your life is unhappy, or if it feels as if something is missing in your life, it may be because you have been fighting who you are—swimming upstream, if you will.

## Personal Mission Statement

Many businesses have a Mission Statement that describes the purpose of their company. Discovering your purpose will help you create your own Personal Mission Statement. This statement will be short, powerful, and inspiring, and will cover your personal life, work, social life, and spiritual life. These literally will be words to live by. As we said before, your life purpose is based upon Who you are. Who you are is based upon your values, talents, gifts, and desires. By close examination of who you are, we will create your Personal Mission Statement which will tell you the purpose of your life. The following assessment will require some insightful self-examination on your part. The result of your assessments will far outweigh the effort it takes to complete them.

## Life Values

The following are a list of Life Values, which reflect human nature. Go through the list carefully and circle 5 Life Values, which

BEST reflect who you are. Do not thing about what SHOULD be your values. Think about and choose the values which will best reflect the impact you would like to make on the world, or the value that you would like to be best known for. (Note: we all have many of these values in different amounts. We are looking for the values for you that exist in the greater abundance and that excite you when you think about them.)

Use the Categories on the left side to help you narrow your search. The Values are on the right-hand side. You can choose from these values, use them to jar your imagination for values of your own, or simply add the values to the list that you feel are missing.

| Categories | Life Values |
| --- | --- |
| **Adventure:** | risk, danger, thrill, quest, experiment, speculation, excitement, the unknown |
| **Beauty:** | loveliness, elegance, taste, grace, culture, attractiveness |
| **Movement:** | spark, motivate, stimulate, coach, influence, energize, move forward, free others, impact, infuse |
| **Contribution:** | serve, improve, strengthen, grant, assist, minister to, provide, facilitate |
| **Creation:** | design, invent, build, inspire, assemble, plan, perfect, imagination |
| **Discovery:** | perceive, uncover, observe, detect, locate, learn |

**Feelings:** sense, be in touch with, to feel good, energy flow, emote, passion

**Leadership:** inspire, influence, model, persuade, reign, cause, guide, exemplify, model

**Mastery:** expert, rule field, superiority, excellence, set standards, the extraordinary

**Pleasure:** have fun, sensual, be entertained, bliss, play games, sex, sports

**Relating:** be connected, part of community, family, be with, to nurture, to unite

**Sensitivity:** tenderness, show compassion, touch, support, empathize, perceive

**Spirituality:** be aware, relate with God, holy, religious, devoting, honoring, awake

**Teaching:** educate, inform, instruct, prepare, enlighten, explain, knowledge

**Winning:** prevail, accomplish, attain, win over, acquire, score, triumph

Look over your 5 circled choices of Life Values. Now you must consider them carefully, comparing two at a time and deciding which one suits your life better. The idea here is to narrow down to one choice of Life Values that best reflects you.

## The one Life Value that best reflects you is:

_____.

## Personal Impact

The next thing we have to discover in your Personal Mission Statement is Who or What you are supposed to interact with in fulfilling your life purpose.

In choosing from the list below, choose the one group of people or things that you would most like to impact in your life. Circle your choice or add your own.

ADD
Abused
Addicts
Adults
Afraid
Afflicted
Alone
Animals
Artists
Athletes
Audiences
Business people
Challenged
Children
Couples
Creatives
Cultures
Depressed
Disabled
Disorganized
Dying
Elderly

Entrepreneurs
Environment
Families
Forgotten
Foster Children
Homeless
Hungry
Illiterate
Inexperienced
Jobless
LBGTQ
Managers
Married
Men
Mentally Ill
Migrants
Minorities
Multiple Sclerosis
Non-believers
Poor
Political
Professionals

Retirees

Rich

Senior Citizens

Sick

Single Parents

Singles

Sinners

Small Business Owners

Spiritual

Uneducated

Unfaithful

Uninspired

Widows/Widowers

Women

Workers in a particular field

Working Class

Writers

Young Adults

Other Group Not Listed

_____

**The group of people or things that you would most like to impact in your life are:**

_____

## Main Actions

The last choice you have to make in order to compose your Personal Mission Statement is the Main Action or Actions you will take in order to impact your chosen group of people or things, while upholding your Life Value. Base your Main Action choices on those things you love to do or choose words that describe your talents, gifts, or passions.

You may find that you want to add a noun or descriptive word after the action words below. For example, if you chose the word "Acting," you may feel a desire to add something to it such as "Acting on Broadway," etc. This is perfectly acceptable and may even help to narrow your choices. Circle two Main Action choices from the list below or add your own.

Achieving

Acting

Adapting

Admitting

Affirming

Aiding

Analyzing

Assembling

Beautifying
Building
Caring For
Changing
Coaching
Collecting
Connecting
Cooking
Consulting
Cultivating
Creating
Dancing
Decorating
Defeating
Demonstrating
Destroying
Devoting
Discovering
Drawing
Driving
Eating
Embracing
Entertaining
Evaluating
Exploring
Feeding
Fighting
Fishing
Flying
Growing
Guiding
Hiking
Influencing

Informing
Infusing
Inspiring
Leading
Listening
Massaging
Motivating
Painting
Photographing
Planting
Playing
Preserving
Relating
Remaining
Remodeling
Renewing
Restoring
Running
Sailing
Sculpting
Selling
Sharing
Singing
Speaking
Spending Time
Sports (specific sport)
Swimming
Talking
Teaching
Touching
Transforming
Traveling
Walking

Working                                   Others Not Listed:
Writing
_____

**My Main Action choices are:**

_____

**Composing your Personal Mission Statement**

1. First fill in the corresponding blanks below with your choices from above

- My chosen Life Value is _____

- My chosen Group of People or Things I most want to impact is: _____

- My chosen Main Actions are: _____

2. Now using your three choices, create a draft statement (combining all three) which has the true ring of what you are meant to do in this life:

_____

_____

3. Now complete this statement: the benefit that the world will receive from my purpose in life is:

_____

4. Refine your statement with another draft. You may want to add the benefit your purpose has for the world to your statement. Make sure your statement reflects your passions and purpose.

_____

_____

5. Now you are ready to make final adjustments and write your true version of your Personal Mission Statement.

**My Personal Mission Statement/Purpose in Life is:**

_____

_____

Once you have composed your Personal Mission Statement/ Life Purpose, you must realize that it is time to re-analyze and sometimes change your existing goals. It is your job in this life to fulfill your purpose. This is the reason you have a purpose. And please do not think that you to wait for everything to become crystal clear of the how's and why's of fulfilling your purpose. You should begin to move in that direction immediately. Take one step at a time in that direction, even when you don't yet see where it is leading. Your vision will clarify as you progress forward. I invite you to go through the process of this booklet and revise or review your results from time to time in order to help your vision become as clear as possible. Does finding your purpose mean that you must throw out your entire life and start over? No, of course not. Your life purpose is not necessarily what you do to make a living. You must determine this. There are risks involved at different levels, but you must take them in order to live your dreams.

Answer the questions below to assist you in planning your life, based on your Life Purpose.

Ask yourself, "What three changes would I make in my life immediately in order to fully honor and express my life purpose?" Write them down.

1.

2.

3.

Ask yourself, "What three changes will I make in the next 90 days in order to fully honor and express my life purpose?" Write them down.

1.

2.

3.

Ask yourself, "What three changes will I make in the next 5 years in order to fully honor and express my life purpose?" Write them down.

1.

2.

3.

Ask yourself, "When I am fully honoring and expressing my life purpose, what will my life look like?" Take a moment and fill in the section below with a written picture of perfectly fulfilled life purpose.

Knowing your life purpose will be source of deep joy to you. Your confusion will begin to fade, and you will have a truer direction. Once you have a direction, you will know which way to walk. It makes life simpler. Fulfilling your life purpose requires commitment and perseverance. It won't be easy. And yet, up until now, you may have lived your life by chance. Is there a better way to live your life than ON PURPOSE?

I sincerely hope that this test will help guide you towards your destiny and true happiness.

Love,

Jax

# ACKNOWLEDGMENTS

What in the world would I do without my readers? I want to say thank you to you all for your readership, your encouragement, and your gumbeaux-ship! Do you know what I love best about you? You're hilarious! You send in the funniest story ideas for new Gumbeaux Sistahs adventures. Some of them are pure doozies, and I hope you keep sending them. I wish I had room enough between the front and back book covers to include them all, but of course, I don't. But I did manage to sneak in a few. You know who you are, and to you I say - thank you, thank you, thank you!

I also want to thank Elizabeth Frey, my unrelenting and adored editor. I want to thank Sharon Brown, owner of the Natchez Coffee Co., for serving the community of Natchez and for allowing me to sit at one of her tables every day, to write and write and write. Also, many thanks go to my Gumbeaux Sistahs groups for advance reading and sussing out plot holes, weak spots, and my penchant for waaaay more than enough commas.

Since my last book, I bought a home in Natchez, Mississippi in order to have a place to lie low during hurricane season. Now I will be splitting my time between Natchez and New Orleans. Of course, my heart will always be in my hometown, but Natchez is a very cool place. It sort of feels like a compact New Orleans. They even occasionally refer to their city as The Little Easy. They have awesome people, beautiful antebellum homes, and they even have a not-to-be-missed Hot Air Balloon festival. It's been an adventure living in my new city, and what's better than a new adventure? As they say, "Life is short, eat the gumbeaux!"

Gumbeaux on, sistahs!

Jax

# ABOUT THE AUTHOR

**Jax Frey**

orn in New Orleans, Jax Frey came into this world with a sense of celebration of culture, food, family, and fun. Translating that celebration into her writing and onto canvas is her true calling. Her colorful art depicts everything Louisiana from her dancing *Gumbeaux Sistahs* paintings to her popular line of original Mini paintings. Over 30,000 original mini paintings have been created and sold into art collections worldwide, and Jax holds a World Record for *The Most Original Acrylic Paintings on Canvas by One Artist.*

Jax splits her time between New Orleans and Natchez, MS and can be found writing in her favorite local coffeehouses everyday with her loveable, tornado-of-a-pug named Lucy, along with Lucy's new sidekick, Ethel.

**Contact Jax** for her available dates for book signings,
zoom meetings, and speaking engagements.
Sign up for the *Gumbeaux Sistahs* newsletter
at www.gumbeauxsistahs.com
FB and Instagram: **Gumbeaux Sistahs**
Jax's art can be seen at: www.artbyjax.com
Facebook and Instagram; **Jax Frey**

# WE LOVE REVIEWS!

Dear Readers:

Please share your reading experience of *The Gumbeaux Sistahs* novels:

- o Help others make good book choices
- o Help your authors get the word out about their work.

*Simply leave a review of your favorite*
Gumbeaux Sistahs *novel on Amazon.*

Here's how to leave a review:

- Just go to www.amazon.com and search for *The Gumbeaux Sistahs*
- Click on your favorite *Gumbeaux Sistahs* book title.
- Scroll down to find the "Review This Product" section to leave your review.

Here are some recent reviews to give you an example. The review can be long or short, it doesn't matter—they are all appreciated and helpful.

*"I LOVED THIS BOOK. I CAN SO RELATE TO THIS BOOK. PEOPLE IN LOUISIANA ARE LIKE THIS. I can't wait to share this book with my own sistahs!"*

*"I absolutely LOVED this book, the style, and description of characters. I went on a cruise and read this book in 1 day! I couldn't put it down. GREAT book, especially if you know the area it takes place in. It's about community, helping one another out and just doing life together. A MUST read in your collection! Oprah needs to endorse it!! Just saying!"*

*"This is a great read for immersing yourself in the fun-loving, warmhearted, feel-good camaraderie that abounds in small Southern towns. The characters are quirky and interesting and find solutions to life's challenges over great gumbo and great wine. Just like my friends and me!"*

**Note: And please copy and paste your Amazon review into your Facebook and Instagram accounts—thanks so very much for the Gumbeaux Sistah love!**

# OTHER BOOKS BY JAX FREY

### *The Gumbeaux Sistahs*
(1st book in *Gumbeaux Sistahs* series)

Five fiery, Southern women wage a hilarious war against the problems of a sistah-in-trouble, using their improbable friendships, unpredictable schemes, oh-so-numerous cocktails, and a shared passion for good gumbo. *The Gumbeaux Sistahs* is a heartwarming, laugh-out-loud story you won't want to put down.

*The Gumbeaux Sistahs is an official selection of the Pulpwood Queens*
*(The largest book club in the world with*
*over 800 book clubs registered)*

### *Gumbeaux Love*
(2nd book in the *Gumbeaux Sistahs* series)

Single, Southern artist Judith Lafferty casually confesses to her Gumbeaux Sistahs that she is occasionally lonely and would like to fall in love again. Seriously— you'd think that by now she would know to keep her mouth shut around these women. The sistahs tackle her problem along with their own love challenges with their usual unreasonable, extreme plots and schemes, including a kidnapping, a cupid costume, and trying out pick-up lines at the deli cheese counter. In helping out their friend, the sistahs help each other as well and bring to light the many flavors of love. Be ready for twists, turns, laugh-out-loud times, and heart-wrenching moments. You'll be sure to recognize yourself and your close friends in the unstoppable sistahs.

## *Gumbeaux Magic*
(3rd Book of the *Gumbeaux Sistahs* series)

Oh my gravy! What's next? You never know when life will hit you upside the head, and the Sistahs' tribulations are just getting started. One sistahs is arrested, one is widowed, another is threatened by a younger woman, and yet another is dealing with an attempted abduction! If there is one thing this group of unstoppable women is good at, it's getting together for some amazing gumbo and brainstorming the most unexpected solutions to life's difficulties.

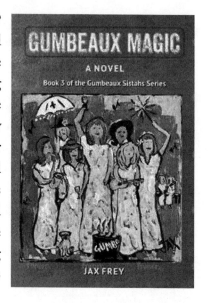

All *Gumbeaux Sistahs* novels are available at **Amazon.com** in paperback and kindle versions.
Order signed copies of books at www.gumbeauxsistahs.com

# Coming Soon

More adventures with the
Gumbeaux Sistahs!

Sign up for the author newsletter to be the first to know when
their next adventure is out at www.gumbeauxsistahs.com

# Free Gift!

Sign up for Gumbeaux Sistahs newsletter to
receive a FREE, emailed, pdf version of

**18 Gumbeaux Sistahs Steps to Living Happily Ever After**

18 Steps that can change your life—try them today!
Visit www.gumbeauxsistahs.com and start
living happily ever after today!

# READERS' GUIDE
## THE GUMBEAUX SISTAHS
## BY JAX FREY

1.  *What three words would you use to best describe this book?*

2.  *What was your favorite moment in the book? Your least favorite?*

3.  *If you were in charge of casting the movie version of this book, who would you cast as each character?*

4.  *If you could invite one character over to your house for dinner, who would it be & why?*

5.   *If you had to trade places with any character in the book, who would you choose & why?*

6.   *What surprised you the most when you were reading this book?*

7.   *How did the setting of the book impact the story?*

8.   *If you had to choose one lesson that the author was trying to teach us with this story, what would it be?*

10.   *If you could write one more chapter after the ending, what would you write?*

*<u>Ethel and Lucy</u>*
**Painting by Alisha Herd**

Made in the USA
Middletown, DE
03 March 2023

25989190R00128